The Box of Secrets

A Tale of Mystery and History from
the American Revolution

D1418412

H. D. Walker

HARMONY HIVE PUBLISHERS
WILTON, NEW HAMPSHIRE

Note From the Author

This book is dedicated to George Washington and those who have served in America's military to win and then preserve the freedoms we have in America. This book is particularly dedicated to George Washington Oestreich II and his wife, Francis Mikels Oestreich. Mr. Oestreich served in the United States Army as a chaplain in the Pacific theater during World War II. He and his wife then served in Japan after the war as missionaries for thirty-three years. Mr. Oestreich passed away at the age of 101 on August 29, 2018. Francis had predeceased him back in March of 2018. They have been tremendous examples to many including myself over the last forty-five years. They also allowed me to marry their daughter Jeannette for which I am deeply thankful.

CONTENTS

1

Buying a Box

Nothing makes my heart skip a beat the way the shrill voice of the auctioneer sounds while he plies his trade. His voice is loud and high-pitched and always has a sense of urgency. It makes me want to buy something. I knew I couldn't. I was only a thirteen-year-old girl. I was only here to watch. That's okay though. People-watching is a hobby of mine. That was how our adventure started.

"The next item for bid is going to whet your appetite for mystery and awaken your spirit of adventure. Yes folks, it is this antique trunk. Isn't she a beauty! We don't have an exact date for it, but the early 1800s would be about right. It came in just this morning, and we haven't been able to open it yet. There are items inside that may be of value, so you could say this is a possible treasure chest. At the very least, it would make a great hope chest for some young lady." With that the auctioneer winked at me. I always felt uncomfortable when someone winked at me. I knew it was his job to be friendly, but I still felt odd about it. I turned to Gramps who was sitting next to me.

"Oh Gramps, I could refinish the trunk and put my tennis rackets and sports equipment in it." I loved competition and came by that attitude honestly since Gramps was the same way. I didn't usually ask Gramps for stuff. I would much rather save up for something and then it would feel like I really deserved it. This was different though. Auction items could be unique and gone before you know it. Besides, if Gramps bought it I would pay him back.

"That trunk is certainly not a 'beauty,' Greta. It definitely needs refinishing. I don't think they even dusted it off before bringing it out here. However, your folks would love for you to have your equipment squared away. We shall see what we can do, but don't get your hopes up. There may be others here who want that trunk, too."

"Let's start the bidding at $20," called the auctioneer. "Would you give $20, would you go twenty, would you bid twenty for it?" There was no response to this first call, so the auctioneer made the next logical move. "How about ten? Would you give $10, would you go ten, would you bid ten for it? Right there is a gentleman who knows a good buy." The auctioneer was pleased to get the first bid and pointed to a man three rows back and to my right. I turned my head slightly to the bidder wearing a short-sleeved shirt with glasses and an iPhone stuffed in his pocket. I thought he looked like an accountant who should have more than $10 to pay for an antique.

"How about fifteen?" bellowed the auctioneer. "Would you give $15, would you go fifteen, would you bid fifteen for it?"

I had always been impressed by how fast the auctioneer could speak ever since Gramps started taking me to these events. Leaning over I whispered to Gramps, "Sure would like to have that trunk in my room." Gramps seemed to wince a little. He was careful with his finances and especially wary of a sale.

The auctioneer nodded to a lady in the front row on our right.

"I have $25 now." The lady looked middle-aged and was smartly dressed. I could imagine she traveled to Europe every year with enough clothes in trunks to fill the *Titanic* with. Why did she want this trunk? It wasn't fair.

"How about thirty?" was the cry. "Would you give $30, would you go thirty, would you bid thirty for it?"

Gramps hesitated for a moment and then signaled he was in for $30. Another man then bid $35. He was a big man with watermelon shoulders. I thought he looked like a lumberjack. I could just picture him chopping up the trunk to use for firewood at his camp. Gramps had to go forty to stay in the game. He also whispered to me that it was his last bid. The competition said $45 and it seemed to be over when the auctioneer called for $50 and then pointed to a new bidder.

Both Gramps and I froze in our seats when we realized at the same time that my hand was up. The auctioneer quickly closed the deal with, "Going once, going twice, sold to the young lady for $50."

"I suppose I am in for the $40," Gramps admitted with a smile. "Did you bring $10, or do I have to float you a loan?" He pretended to be annoyed, but I saw through his ruse and gave him that puppy-dog look with upturned lips that always melted him. The simple truth was that he enjoyed these little predicaments which gave him the chance to tease his granddaughter.

I call him Gramps, but his actual name is Joshua Webb. Gramps doesn't play favorites and likes to think that he loves all his grandkids equally. He admits, though, that he and I seem to have a great number of common interests. We both love new experiences. I enjoy his company very much. To me he doesn't seem old or out of touch. I learn a lot from him. We really treat each other with mutual respect.

Gramps had recently retired from a career in computer software security. He had enjoyed his work but felt life still had much to be explored. Learning was a lifelong love, and if that could be done alongside one of his grandkids then it was all the more enjoyable. From time to time he found himself in situations like buying an old trunk at auction. He tried to turn those occasions into educational experiences. Often Gramps realized that he was the one doing the learning.

When the auction ended I bounded from my seat toward the aisle and tripped over a chair. "Ow, that smarts," I said.

"Whoa, kiddo," said Gramps. "That trunk isn't going anywhere till we pay for it, so there's no need to hurry."

I really couldn't help myself. Whenever Gramps and I went places it felt like an adventure, so I practically raced to claim my box before the auctioneer could change his mind. It probably wasn't a treasure, I told myself, but little did we know what the next few weeks were going to bring. Gramps and I were about to begin a journey that we would never forget. Whether you called this an adventure, or a journey, or a mystery didn't really matter to me. We were going to take a walk through history. We were going to make discoveries that were truly shocking. Talk about mystery. Talk about treasure. The auction was where it all started.

*   *   *

Later that day we carried the old trunk into the house Gramps and Gram shared. It was a modest home as far as architecture went, but Gram had put her unmistakable mark of hospitality and hard

work into it. She was away now helping my Aunt Becky with the
birth of her third child. After fourteen grandchildren this was
a duty Gram relished, and the family assumed and appreciated.
Gram's real name is Julie Webb, but I just call her Gram.

My parents were on a trip to the United Kingdom celebrating
their twentieth anniversary. It didn't take much convincing for
me to stay with Gramps while they were away. We liked to do
things together. We also liked pizza with sausage and black olives
and extra cheese. He had taught me how to play tennis, and
even though I made the high school team, he was still very stiff
competition for me.

Skipper began to bark as if cheering us on to carry the box.
Skipper had all the marking of a West Highland Scottish Terrier.
It would be diplomatic to call Skipper a Westie, though, since the
dog's pedigree was far from settled. Skipper had no papers, but
Gramps didn't seem to mind. He and Gram had fallen in love with
the dog for numerous reasons. The clear fact was that Skipper had
more energy than a whirling dervish and loved to get in on any
action going on around him. That energy and the white mustache
made him much like his master.

We set the heavy box down in the living room with a dull clunk.
If the auctioneer was right then the trunk might very well be
over two hundred years old. It was made of real wood and was
held together by wood strips and metal brackets. The metal was
tarnished and the wood was in great need of refinishing. The
remains of what used to be leather handles were attached to the
sides. They were broken, which was most likely caused by age and
heavy loads. On top of the box toward the front was a metal plate
stamped with the initials RT.

"I wonder who those initials belonged to," mumbled Gramps.

Now the real problem was to get this old trunk open and see what was inside. Gramps got his tools and began to fidget with the metal lock on the front of the box. After a few minutes, he looked at me with a silly grin. "Now you know why I was a software engineer and not into hardware. If it can't be done with duct tape or WD-40 then I am at a loss."

"I have confidence in you, Gramps. If anyone can get it open, you can." I said that in such a way that Gramps knew I was trying to butter him up. That was okay since Gramps loved it when I buttered him up. I knew he would keep trying.

"A glass of lemonade would go a long way toward getting this trunk open," he said. I nodded and went to the kitchen to see what was in the fridge.

A knock at the door surprised us both. The house was out on the edge of the woods, so visitors didn't come that often. We were not expecting anyone today. I opened the door to find two men whom I had never seen before. They were both wearing somewhat dirty T-shirts so they did not fit the picture of salesmen.

"Can I help you?" I asked politely. Skipper began to softly growl in his throat. "Now Skipper, stop that!"

"Are you the girl who bought a trunk at the auction today?" asked the short balding man. Thick-framed glasses fronted his dark beady eyes. His plastic smile offered to sell something that most people would not want to buy.

"Yes, were you at the auction today?"

"No, we just missed it, but we would like to talk to you about the trunk you bought. May we come in?"

By this time Gramps was at the door, too. Out of politeness he said, "By all means, please come in. I am Joshua Webb and this is my granddaughter Greta."

After leading the two men into the living room and once again quieting Skipper, we were all seated and ready to proceed.

"My name is Earle Brubaker, and this is my brother, John Henry. We are antique collectors, and we are interested in the trunk you bought today. Would you be willing to sell it to us? How much would you take for it?"

I almost choked when I heard them say that, but I tried to answer them calmly. "I fell in love with that trunk this morning and have plans for it. I don't want to sell it. Besides, it's the first thing I have ever bought at auction so it makes a memory."

"Well, young lady, it's just an old trunk. There must be a lot of trunks on the market to meet your needs."

Gramps stepped into the conversation, "Why are you so interested in that trunk? It needs to be refinished, and we haven't even been able to open it yet." I knew Gramps was thinking the same thing I was. If these men went to all the trouble to find out who bought the trunk and where we lived, then there must be more to this story than they had revealed. I looked at these men more closely. The way Earle combed his hair over from one side of his head to the other made me smile. He must have been trying to cover up the balding top. The brother was a large man and had a nose that looked like it had been broken on more than one occasion. He reminded me of a pro wrestler I once saw in a video. I think he was called *The Mauler* or *The Marauder* or some such thing.

Earle continued, "We collect antiques and have a spot in our display where that trunk would go nicely. We will give you $100 for it. That's double what you paid. Besides, as you have noticed, it is in rather shabby condition."

I was now agreeing with Skipper's opinion of these men. "I don't think so," I said. "This trunk is rather unique. It's made of cherry wood or something like that. I believe that anything in the store would be very cheap presswood or extremely expensive."

"Okay, let's make it $200," said Earle. "That's a very generous offer."

John Henry burped and then spoke up for the first time. "We *will* get the trunk, so you might as well sell it to us." I could almost feel my cheeks turning red. These men were practically demanding that I sell them the trunk. My blood was beginning to boil and I looked at Gramps to find out what he was thinking.

Gramps began to smile while I felt like growling right along with Skipper. "I will overlook that remark," said Gramps, "which sounded like a threat. If you could tell us the truth about why you are interested, then we might consider your offer."

John Henry looked at Earle as if to ask, should we tell them the truth?

Earle acted like he was ready to confess. "Well, the fact of the matter is the trunk belongs to our Aunt Sadie, and she wants it back. It was mistakenly sent to the auction today. I will still give you the $100, and we can return it to Aunt Sadie."

Gramps smiled again and after a pause said, "I think you offered $200, but I tell you what we will do. Give us your Aunt Sadie's address, and we will return it to her. That trunk appears to have a history, and I would like to find out more about it from her." I could tell that Mr. Bald Guy didn't like this idea.

"But Mr. Webb. You don't know what our aunt is like. She's, she's, well, she's somewhat cantankerous. She doesn't get along with people very well."

"That's okay," I jumped in. "She sounds like someone worth meeting." I figured she must be an improvement over her nephews.

The men looked at each other again and realized that neither Gramps nor I were going to budge from this position. Earle pulled out his pen and wrote the name Sadie Woodruff and an address down on a scrap of paper.

"We could save everyone a lot of trouble by taking it back ourselves, Mr. Webb."

"It's no real trouble. I think we will enjoy meeting your aunt."

A few minutes later, when the men had left, I turned to Gramps and said, "I didn't like them at all."

"No," said Gramps, "neither did I, and what's more, I didn't really believe what they were telling us. It's not a good idea to do business with someone you can't trust. Skipper had the right idea from the beginning. I suspect they are not really antique dealers. I just wish we could get into the trunk and find out the real reason for their interest."

"I don't want to break into it, Gramps, but maybe we should take it to a locksmith. You know a good locksmith, don't you, Gramps?"

"Yes, I have a buddy named Ralph who has a shop down on Elm Street. I am not against taking the trunk to him, but I think the ethical thing to do would be to meet Aunt Sadie first. She may be able to make sense out of what Earle said and John Henry intimated. She may even have a key tucked away in a drawer somewhere. Assuming the address they gave us is correct our GPS indicates it's about twenty-five minutes from here. If she mistakenly put the trunk up for auction, then we should give it back."

I winced and Gramps added, "After getting our $50 back, of course."

I breathed a little sigh and agreed that it would be the right thing to do.

2

The Youthful Spy

W e didn't know what was in Greta's trunk, and I didn't think very much about it at first. Then, after the bizarre visit of the two brothers, I began to study the trunk in a new light. It was a real antique. The 1800s may be the right date after all. We didn't discover until much later that the trunk's story actually began back in 1776. America was set on fire by a spirit of nationalism that was pulling the colonies away from the British yoke. We often hear about the part Boston and Philadelphia played during the Revolution, but New York was a veritable powder keg ready to explode. The British had forced the colonial army out of New York City. As commander-in-chief General George Washington was determined to recapture that strategic area and sent spies into New York to gather intelligence. The early espionage attempts were an utter failure, as I explained to Greta on more than one occasion. Take for example, what happened on September 22, 1776.

* * *

The drum began to beat as the procession slowly made its way down the path to the tree. There were ten men wearing red uniforms and carrying rifles. Four soldiers marched in front of a young man dressed in a suit fit for a church service. There were six who marched behind the prisoner with their rifles at the ready. The prisoner gave no indication that he would give a try for freedom. He appeared completely resigned to his fate. The condemned man was only a few hours from what had been a promising future. He was a Yale College graduate and an officer in Washington's army. Now he was walking to a tree where his final fate would be realized. He looked very pale and had no friend to accompany him on this lonely trek. He had been caught in a business that demanded harsh punishment.

The previous night the prisoner had been sitting in Dove Tavern sipping a mug of cider. A man dressed in buckskin stepped up to his table carrying a pewter plate of stew. He sat down and said, "Ah, my good friend you are alone again I see. Have you had no success in your job hunting? The world does not appreciate the toils of the teaching profession." The newcomer spooned a potato into his mouth and continued.

"Teachers are a necessity but all too often we take them for granted. My own education was on the knee of my dear mother. Well, I do wish you success." There were three men sitting at a table not ten yards away apparently engrossed in their victuals.

"Good sir your company is welcome. My mission is a lonely one." Bending near the rough-clad fellow Nathan Hale spoke softly. "As I intimated yesterday, I am using my eyes and ears more than my mouth. I must learn before I can teach. You seem to know this area well. You must be familiar with what the Redcoats are up to."

The older man leaned forward. "Aye, sir, Indeed I am. I can give you particulars about the nearby garrison with the number of men at arms as well as cannon and horses. I can't help but wonder though, my friend. What does a teacher want with those facts and figures? Is it a teaching position at a military academy you are seeking?"

The young man smiled at this question. Once again he leaned toward his companion. "I feel as though I would burst if I don't tell someone. From what you told me yesterday I know we share common beliefs. Can I trust you, good sir?"

The frontiersman paused for only a moment and then spoke. "Who can be trusted these days?" He began to wave his spoon for emphasis. "You would be surprised by who I am and what I know. In fact I give you my word that my help will make a difference in you achieving your goals."

"Your sincerity touches me deeply. I need your help to uncover information that I need to know. I am on a mission from General Washington himself to find out the strengths and vulnerabilities of the Redcoats. Will you assist me?"

The older man put down his spoon and held out his hand so Nathan could grasp it as a token of friendship. It was then that Nathan realized how strong his companion really was because he could not break the grip. At the same time he felt another hand upon his left shoulder. He started to rise but could not. The three men who had sat nearby now surrounded him. He was powerless in their hold. His mission indeed was at an end.

It was impossible to decide whether Robert Rogers was a hero or a scoundrel. He could best be described as a soldier of fortune. He offered his services to the British as well as the colonies. He had supporters and detractors on both sides. Washington had him arrested at one point which made him ultimately decide to put his talents to the service of the Crown.

Robert Roger's Rangers had been on the lookout the last few days for anything or anyone suspicious. They had seen Patriot ships come near the shore for a brief time as if to drop off a package. After that, this young man had been noticed watching the troops and making notes. He also asked questions that seemed more than just simple curiosity at work. Rogers had approached him at Dove Tavern like a cat sniffing out a mouse and began conversing about his own Patriot sympathies. He then suggested Hale travel with him into the city. The young man took the bait and they arranged to meet the next day.

Espionage could be a lonely work. Perhaps that was why Hale had revealed himself to Rogers. He wanted a friend and confidant and Rogers had seemed so genuine and earnest. The seasoned soldier knew how to string the young man along. Hale thought he could talk to this rough-clad frontiersman and perhaps get help in numbering the British troops and their whereabouts. Rogers brought witnesses the next day as the trap was sprung.

Hale's youth and inexperience had proved his undoing. He had been sent by Washington to get a clear picture of British troop movements in New York City after the Patriots evacuated following the battle of Long Island. He had dressed as a teacher who was looking for employment. It wasn't a good cover story since the school year had already begun.

Hale had incriminating notes on his person that Rogers and his Rangers found. No plausible defense could explain away those notes. Hale was taken to General William Howe. The formality of a trial was dispensed with. The facts were clear and the British general wasted no time sentencing Hale to wear the hangman's noose. Hale was denied his request for a Bible. He was denied seeing a clergyman. He requested writing material which he was furnished with. He wrote one letter to his stepmother and another to a fellow officer. After about twelve hours he joined the solemn procession that led to the hanging tree.

Spies were not respected, even by those in their own ranks. They were considered mercenaries who were willing to lie and steal for gold and favor. Nathan Hale did not fit that description. When Washington pleaded for someone to go behind the British lines on an espionage mission there had initially been no takers. New York had recently fallen to the British invaders. Within a few days of having left the city, Washington began to make plans to return. A key part of those plans was to obtain information about the new occupants. He needed a spy. Nathan Hale stepped forward and said he would go. It was a fateful decision.

He understood his mission and the value of having information about the British troops. The British had the advantages of superior troop numbers as well as naval power that was capable of controlling the waters. New York had a strategic importance because of its location and size and a good number of Tory loyalists. For Washington to return and retake the city information of troops and their movements was vital.

Espionage was not a developed field of study in 1776. Spies were commonly used in warfare throughout history. When the children of Israel were poised to enter the promised land, they sent in twelve men to act as spies. When Homer wrote about the siege of Troy he included accounts of spies being used. From Julius Caesar to Napoleon spies were utilized to collect information. These historical spies acted as scouts by getting close enough to the enemy to learn about the size and movements of opposing armies. Washington himself had performed tasks that were the duties of a spy during the French and Indian war. He knew the value of accurate information to assess enemy strength and movement.

Lieutenant Colonel Thomas Knowlton had interviewed young Nathan to determine his suitability for the mission. Hale was asked if he knew the terrain he would be traveling to and he did not. He had never been to Long Island. He was asked about his battle experience which embarrassed the young man since he had seen very little action. When his unit was fighting in the Boston siege Hale was finishing up the term as a teacher in New London. He had only three things to recommend him for this assignment. First, when he went to Yale, he participated in Dramatical studies. Unfortunately this did not mean playing serious roles but farces meant for entertainment. Second, he had a close friend in Benjamin Tallmadge who knew his character and dedication. Third, and the deciding factor, Hale was the only one willing to take the assignment.

There was no official training at a school for spies that Hale could attend. Yale did not have a course in espionage. He was given words of warning and instructions as to what information was deemed important to the Patriot general. He had a simple cover story for his presence in Long Island. He was to pose as a school master looking for assignment. That in itself was suspicious since schools should have already started with a school master in place. The timing was awkward at best since the British had taken possession of the area only a few days before. He was also running the risk of being seen by friends or relatives who knew him to be of Patriot persuasion.

Young Nathan had graduated with honors from Yale and for a brief time had actually served as a teacher. Then Benjamin

Tallmadge who had been his college classmate inspired him to join the service of his country. Tallmadge and he were very close at Yale and after leaving wrote letters to one another. Tallmadge would simply sign his letters as Damon while Hale would reply using the signature Pythias. Damon and Pythias were characters of Greek mythology known for their friendship. Pythias had plotted to kill King Dionysius and had been arrested for his treachery and sentenced to death. He had requested leave of the king to return home to settle family matters before his execution. Damon had volunteered to take his place and be executed if Pythias did not return. After settling his family affairs Pythias returned to take his just punishment. King Dionysius was so impressed with their friendship he released both of them.

Hale smiled at the thought that no friend could come and take his place right now. Tallmadge would not be able to save him from his fate, but he would play a key role for general Washington in the days ahead.

The procession now stopped before the tree where the rope was attached. Nathan's thoughts wandered to his father Richard who was a devout man. He sent three of his sons to Yale. He would often write to encourage his boys to refrain from mischief and to spend time in God's word. He told them to read a chapter in the Bible every morning and every evening. One of Richard's letters quoted the words of Jesus: "In my fathers house are many mansions, and I go to prepare a place for you". Nathan surely prayed, "Lord Jesus, I am coming soon. I trust you indeed have a place for me." He climbed the ladder before him.

The noose was now circling the young man's neck. As expected, he was given time to address the onlookers. He began to speak in clear tones. "If I had ten thousand lives, I would lay them all down, if called to it, in defense of my injured, bleeding Country. My only regret is that I have but one life to give for my country."

The drum began to beat again and the signal was given. A twenty-one-year-old life came to an end. Nevertheless, the mission continued.

As the crowd disbursed, a young woman was left standing unable to move as yet. She pulled her bonnet snug around her face to cover the tear stains that had left a trail down her cheeks. She had not come for the morbid sense of seeing a hanging. She was there, as a Tory, to show support for the Crown who had punished this young man for his treasonous acts of espionage. Her loyalties had never really been tested before. Now her feelings seemed to have undergone a change. The young man's courage left a deep impression on her. His words showed her there were those who felt America was their country. They were not subject to the Island across the sea. She would never be the same after this sight. She slowly turned and began to make her way toward home.

*   *   *

Nathan Hale's spy career was a brief one. Nevertheless, he left a mark on the Revolutionary War and on his country for years to come. I believe that General Washington learned from that failure and made adjustments. Greta and I were going to learn about the spies Washington used and their contribution to America's quest for freedom.

3

It Happened at Midnight

Gramps had the flashlight in his left hand but he didn't want to turn it on just yet. In his right hand was his trusty five iron. He must have sensed something was wrong downstairs at the same time I did. I watched him inch his way out into the dark hallway moving slowly so as not to make any noise. When he bumped into me we both jumped back with a gasp.

"Gramps, you scared a year's growth right out of me," I whispered. He turned on his flashlight and held his finger up to his lips. Skipper was growling almost imperceptibly in a very low tone. Gramps didn't point his flashlight down the stairs, but we saw some light coming from that direction.

I could feel the hairs on the back of my neck stand up and I whispered, "Did you leave the light on? Because I sure didn't!"

"No, I didn't, and that light seems to be moving like it's a flashlight too. I think someone is in the house besides us," he said.

"Do you think Gram would be home already?," I whispered. I was grasping for any explanation other than the obvious.

"No, she isn't due for another week, and she would have called if her plans had changed that much." Skipper continued to softly

growl as we inched toward the top of the stairs. The three of us stopped in our tracks and strained to listen.

We heard a voice say, "Careful with your end. Don't drop it." We froze in place. I looked at Gramps and my eyes must have been as bright as diamonds.

"This is heavier than I expected," said another voice. "Do you think it really has something valuable inside it?"

"I am certain of it. We are paying Detective Dolittle a pretty penny to find out what Aunt Sadie has been hiding all these years. That old crow has her hands on a fortune, and I aim to make sure she doesn't squander it."

The second voice responded with, "I still can't believe she would just send this trunk out to be auctioned off. Maybe she really has lost her marbles."

"Quiet down. You don't want to wake them or the dog."

All at once Skipper started yelping as if his tail was on fire and raced down the stairs and into the dining room. Gramps and I heard a loud frightened scream followed by a heavy thunk and the sound of feet running to the front door.

I started to run down the stairs, but Gramps held me back for a few moments and softly said, "Let's give our friends the chance to make their exit." Then we both scrambled gingerly down the stairs and turned on the outside light in time to watch two figures move swiftly down the driveway and hop into a Ford F150 truck. The engine roared to life and the truck squealed its tires getting away.

"Gramps, there were two men," I spewed out excitedly while trying to catch my breath.

"Yes, I know. And I think they were more frightened than we were. Skipper did a great job sending them on their way. That dog, pound for pound, is something else. He just proved the old axiom, 'It's not the size of the dog in the fight that matters. It's the size of the fight in the dog.'"

"Oh Gramps, my heart is still racing. I really did lose a year's growth. I think I am only four foot two now." I gave him my most sincere look for about three seconds, and then couldn't help laughing. "Noooooottttttttt. So, who were those men, Gramps?"

"Well, I am not positive, but my best guess is they were Earle and John Henry whom we met today." We both immediately turned to look at the trunk lying in the middle of the room.

"That trunk was over against the wall when we hit the sack tonight," I said. "Now look where it is. So that thunk we heard was them dropping the trunk when Skipper sailed to the rescue."

"It would appear so," agreed Gramps. "That bears out my theory that this trunk may hold a lot more than what those two were telling us."

"What are we going to do now?," I asked. "We haven't been able to open it yet, and I don't want to break it open."

"I think the best thing to do would be to stick to our original plan, and visit this Sadie Woodruff and see if she is anything like her two nephews. From what I heard those two say, she isn't on the best of terms with them. However, in answer to your question, right now we are going to secure the doors. I am sure I locked the doors last night, but I don't think I used the deadbolt." Gramps proceeded to check and lock every door in the house.

"I believe a cup of hot chocolate would give us a good way to make the best of this time. What do you say, kiddo? I don't think those two will be coming back tonight."

"That all sounds great — especially the hot chocolate. Maybe we can give Skipper a cookie?"

"Now you're talking," said Gramps. "I will put some water on to heat and perhaps you can find the cocoa mix in the cupboard."

A few minutes later, we were warming our hands around steaming mugs of cocoa.

"You make a good cup of cocoa," said Gramps. "I knew Gram was leaving me in good hands with you."

"My heart is still racing," I said. "I have never been so scared in my life. Do you think we should call the police?"

"I have been considering that. I think those two are amateur burglars at best or they would not have made such a racket. If confronted they would simply deny it, and we would have to admit that we did not get a clear look at them to be certain of who it was. Besides all that, it is one o'clock in the morning, and I don't really want to make a report right now. Perhaps we will tomorrow."

"I second that, Gramps. I don't want to stay up right now and answer twenty questions. What do you think is so valuable about that trunk? Even if it is from the 1800s, it isn't in good enough shape to be considered valuable. There must be something inside it that Earle and John Henry consider worthwhile."

"It's hard to tell without opening it," said Gramps. "To be honest with you, I would rather not know. If it is something truly valuable in terms of money, then I don't want to be tempted by it. If it is something that Aunt Sadie would really rather keep, then I want to get it back to her as soon as possible. We don't want to buy into someone else's affairs. Tomorrow, or should I say later today, since it is well past midnight, we need to go see this Aunt Sadie. Right now we need to finish our cocoa and go get some rest. What do you say?"

"I wish Dad and Mom were here. I got a letter from them yesterday describing their visit to Stonehenge. I am so glad they are having a good time. I hate telling them about burglars when they are gone. They won't like me having been in any danger."

"I don't think we were in any real danger, but I will be reviewing the security of our home. This has always been a safe neighborhood. It's just odd that an old beat-up trunk could cause someone to come and break in. However, those two were not exactly the sharpest knives in the drawer. When you write to your folks, you needn't mention a burglary. We shouldn't spoil their vacation. They can't do anything about it from England anyway. You can fill them in when they get back."

"I have been thinking about the initials RT on the box, Gramps. Who could it have been?"

"That's a great question, kiddo. It is either the craftsman who made the box or the person who the box was made for. If we knew who RT was, then we would have a better understanding of the trunk's value. Well, we won't learn any more about it until we talk to this Aunt Sadie or get the box open."

"You have to admit that this sure seems like a mystery. I have been reading a lot of mystery stories, and this has all the markings of one. Have you ever been in a mystery before, Gramps?"

"No, I can't say as I have. Those two didn't seem mysterious, though. If the trunk was valuable and they knew about it they should have communicated better with their aunt. It should never have been shipped out of the house. I would describe them as bungling instead of mysterious."

"I will definitely keep Skipper in my room tonight. Then I should be able to get some sleep."

"Sounds good, kiddo. Sleep tight and don't let the bed bugs bite."

"Toodles, Gramps."

It wasn't easy for me to get to sleep that night. I kept calling out to Skipper to make sure he was there. After a while it was obvious that Skipper was smarter than I was, since he was sleeping. I closed my eyes and wished for morning.

*   *   *

Twenty miles away, a Ford F150 with two men inside pulled into a driveway. "We sure messed that up," the passenger said.

"What do you mean we? You were talking loud enough to wake the dead. Why can't you learn to keep quiet?"

"Don't blame me. I warned you about the dog. Was it a German Shepherd that attacked us, do you think?"

"You idiot, that was no shepherd. It was some kind of terrier."

"It's a good thing for them that dog didn't bite. I would have sued them for a pretty penny. Now what are we going to do about getting the trunk?"

"We are not going to break into their house again. We will have to rely on Detective Dolittle. Maybe he can steal it for us."

"Good thinking. We can give him a call in the morning."

4

The Soldier Spy

October 11, 1776

All was calm now save for the gentle lapping of the water against the ship. Discovery would prove costly. The ragtag crew must hold their own against the finest navy and army in the world. They were outgunned and out-manned. Their only hope lay in the audacity of surprise and the grit to remain quiet. Every sailor understood their precarious position. Their fleet consisted of fifteen small ships constructed in haste over the last two months to face the British Armada of thirty-four vessels of varying sizes. The Americans were led by Benedict Arnold who knew the lake better than any other commander involved in this action, and he had a plan. The small fleet under Arnold's command was waiting in the channel between Valcour Island and the colony of New York on the western side of Lake Champlain.

The wind was brisk from north to south and the British sailed past the island never suspecting any ruse. No scouting vessels were sent to locate the American fleet. The American captains held a last-minute planning session aboard Commander Arnold's ship *Congress*.

"Gentlemen, the wind will be at our backs and our smaller ships will be able to change course in a moment," stated Commander Arnold. "Remind your officers to cover powder barrels with blankets to guard against sparks, and it would be well to sprinkle sand on your ship's decks."

"But, Commander Arnold, why sprinkle the sand?"

Arnold smiled and then replied, "to avoid slipping in the blood, sir."

As soon as the captains returned to their vessels, the American fleet was under way. A yellow flag was flying from each ship with a picture of a rattlesnake and the words, "Don't Tread on Me." When British General Guy Carleton aboard his flagship *Maria* saw they had been tricked, he was disturbed. Now the wind was against them. They were forced to tack back to the north and fight the wind as well as the Americans.

The Americans opened fire as the British began to maneuver for position. The Royal Navy returned fire, and one well aimed shot hit the mast of the *Royal Savage*, which was the largest American vessel. The ship lost control and hit rocks causing it to capsize. The crew quickly abandoned ship and took to the forest.

Arnold was not content to observe and give orders. He began scurrying around his ship aiming the cannon and firing at the targets. One shot came close to striking General Carleton himself. The general tried to remain calm, but this must have been more than he expected. The powder magazine on one British ship was hit and exploded in a rain of fire. From the shore, Indians, who were allied with the British, began shooting at the Patriot sailors. American marksmen climbed up the masts and began to fire back. Boarding parties got in small boats to row toward the American ships only to have their boats blown out of the water.

The battle was heavy and both sides were taking punishment. Fighting raged on through the afternoon. As the light began to fade, the American fleet took refuge in the channel and prepared for the worst. Carleton set the *Royal Savage* on fire, which lit up the sky. It was obvious to Arnold that the British were ready to call it a night. Once again Commander Arnold called for a meeting of his remaining captains.

"Gentlemen, I believe we have just three options from our present position. First, we can fight them bravely as we did today. Our ammunition is not as plentiful as theirs, and we will be blown from the water. Second, we can send General Carleton an emissary offering our surrender." Arnold waited for a response from his officers.

"You said there is a third option, Commander Arnold?"

"Yes, I believe there is. Tonight is a moonless night. The British have larger ships than we, and they do not know this shoreline. They are offshore further than they need to be out of caution. There is room to maneuver our smaller ships between the British fleet and the western shore and then make a run for it."

"Good heavens, man! Can we do it?"

"It will require the utmost discipline and courage. After what I saw of the men today, I believe we can do it."

"What is your plan, Commander?"

"We will have to wait till midnight when the night watchmen are most drowsy. Each ship will have to row with shirts wrapped around the oars to quiet them. The only light will be placed on the rear of each ship and partially covered so as not to be visible from the east. Your men must be silent as the grave. Yes, gentlemen, we can do it."

"Commander Arnold, it just might work."

And work it did. When dawn broke the next morning the Americans were all gone. Carleton was livid. Once again he had been made a fool of by underestimating the ingenuity of Benedict Arnold. He immediately ordered his ships to give chase. It was thirty-five miles to Crown Point, where Patriot artillery was expected to be. The American fleet had gone about eight miles when the British began the pursuit. The American ships were badly in need of repairs. By a combination of sailing and rowing through a second sleepless night, the runaways were still about twenty miles from Crown Point when the British war ships began closing in. Once again Commander Arnold made a daring decision and ordered the remaining ships to beach themselves on the rocks. The shallow waters meant the larger British ships could not approach. Disembarking with their wounded, the Patriots set the ships on fire. They proceeded to Crown Point on foot and then on to Fort Ticonderoga.

The soldiers at Fort Ticonderoga were frightened when they learned that General Carleton's army was on the way. There was a shortage of supplies and ammunition. They feared they could not withstand an attack. No attack came. It was almost two weeks after Arnold's arrival at Fort Ticonderoga that General Carleton came within sight. He studied the fort but did not approach within cannon fire. It seemed that Carleton had enough fighting for the time being. Perhaps he was unsure of his supply lines. Winter would be setting in soon. He may not have wanted to risk being surprised a third time by his unpredictable adversaries. He could make his report that he had defeated the American forces in two actions. He decided to return to Canada and set up winter quarters.

Benedict Arnold had built and then sunk the first American naval armada. He had caused enough alarm for the king's army and navy to wait for a better day to fight. The Hudson was now frozen over and safe from attack till the following spring.

*   *   *

The courage of Benedict Arnold was never in question. Even though he distinguished himself in battle on land and on the water, he had a knack for making enemies. His military exploits were only surpassed by his political foibles. While his ships were being constructed for the Battle of Valcour Island, he was requested to appear before a military court at Ticonderoga to defend himself of accusations that he had robbed merchants in Quebec. In his appearance, he showed utter contempt for the proceedings prompting the judges to demand that he apologize. He said he would be only too happy to give the judges "satisfaction" after the court concluded its business. In other words he was challenging all the judges to a duel. General Horatio Gates, who was in charge of the American military in the area, was forced to intervene and disband the court so Arnold could return to the work at hand — the war.

After the Battle of Valcour Island had halted the advance of the British down the Hudson for a season, Benedict Arnold was somewhat of a celebrity. He read his own praises in the papers and received prominent visitors who expressed admiration.

There was also a growing jealousy between politicians and the military. Some members of Congress were noticing that the military was getting the praises of the people above the politicians. They were concerned about the popularity of Washington as well as Arnold. In the midst of this background Washington requested

Congress to appoint five new major generals and wanted Arnold to be one of them. When the appointments were made, however, Arnold was not among them. It was an affront that would plague the relationship between Arnold, Washington, and Congress for the remainder of the war.

Arnold engaged in a feud with Congress over his promotion to major general. While Congress eventually gave him the promotion after heroic exploits in Connecticut, he was now junior in rank to the five who had received the recognition before him. He petitioned Congress for seniority, but his lobbying efforts in Philadelphia were poorly constructed. He became bitter, and on July 11, 1777, submitted his resignation.

The British were invading from the north and Washington sent a letter to Congress the same day Arnold submitted his resignation. Arnold was needed in upper New York. He was asked to withdraw his resignation and go north to fight the enemy. The one thing Arnold craved more than glory was action. His rather illustrious saga was still in its early stages.

*　　　*　　　*

British General John Burgoyne had taken Fort Ticonderoga and was preparing to move toward Albany with about eight thousand soldiers. He expected to split New England off from the rest of the colonies. Burgoyne was confident he would have the war won in less than a year. The American army had six thousand troops and was continually being added to as new volunteers arrived almost daily. They harassed the British force with delaying tactics — blocking paths and destroying bridges.

General Arnold arrived and reported to Philip Schuyler. Another

British force commanded by Barry St. Leger with 750 Redcoats and perhaps a thousand Mohawk braves was advancing from the west. They were now laying siege to Fort Stanwix in the Mohawk Valley. Schuyler believed that the western enemy must be prevented from joining Burgoyne. He asked for a volunteer to lead a Patriot force to relieve Fort Stanwix and defend against the Mohawks. Arnold stepped forward. He was put in command of a volunteer army of nine hundred, or about half the size of St. Leger's troops.

August 21, 1777

When Arnold approached the enemy, he wanted to attack at once. They were heavily outnumbered, so his officers urged him to send for help. Arnold set up headquarters in a small cabin. A mother pushed into the cabin and pleaded for the life of her son. The young man, named Hon Yost, had been recruiting Loyalists to serve in the British Army. He had been tried for treason and sentenced to death. The mother begged for his life and Arnold reluctantly agreed to talk with the condemned man.

Arnold was facing a major dilemma against a superior British force that must be stopped. He now had a nagging problem of dealing with a mother who begged him to spare her son. He conceived an audacious plan to use one problem to solve the other. He told Hon Yost that he would spare him if he performed a mission and the young man agreed. They took the young man's coat off and shot several bullet holes in it. They then sent him in the direction of St. Leger's camp.

Yost ran into the British camp where several Mohawk warriors prepared to shoot him. The young man frantically held up his hands and pointed to the holes in his coat. He said he had luckily escaped from the Patriots. He excitedly proclaimed that Benedict Arnold was on his way with a huge American army. There were as many Patriots as there were leaves on the trees. The Mohawks had heard enough. They were brave warriors but not disciplined soldiers. This siege was not to their liking. The Redcoats could sit and wait, but not them. They rushed about in a frenzy saying the British were setting them up to be butchered. Grabbing supplies they ran away in a panic. It wasn't long before many British regulars followed suit. St. Leger had no choice now but to retreat to Canada. Arnold arrived at Fort Stanwix on August 24. The Americans there gave him the news. The British and Mohawk invaders had vanished. Han Yost had fulfilled his mission.

September 19, 1777

Schuyler was replaced as lead general by Horatio Gates. General Arnold had gotten along well with Gates the previous year at Valcour Island since they were geographically separated. Arnold's naval experience prompted Gates to let him be independent at that time. The current situation was very different. Gates thought Arnold was rash and could not be trusted.

General Gates wanted to take up a defensive position and let the enemy come to him while Arnold's attitude was always to attack. Arnold believed they could use the rugged terrain to their advantage. Staff meetings became hot argument sessions so Gates quit inviting Arnold to attend.

The Americans had set up defensive positions around Saratoga, and Gates was daring the British to approach. As the Redcoats came closer, the Patriots could hear the beating of their drums.

Burgoyne was counting on the Americans to sit and wait, so he was pushing his cannon to the front to bombard Gates's position. Arnold pleaded with Gates to let him lead a force against the advancing enemy. Gates reluctantly agreed and Arnold led a regiment of two thousand men against the British in a field on Freeman's farm. Arnold's bravery inspired his men in the fight.

Daniel Morgan was an officer in Arnold's regiment and, with a company of sharpshooters, climbed trees and began to shoot at the British officers. The battle raged on the farm as first the British and then the Patriots took control of the field. For three hours the scene was one of carnage as the combatants poured a withering fire on one another.

Arnold charged around the field on his black stallion shouting, "Come on boys" to his men. He sent message after message to Gates calling for reinforcements. Gates stood safely by his tent listening to the sounds of cannon and gunfire.

Gates finally recalled Arnold from the field and the British took possession of Freeman's farm and claimed victory. The casualty count favored the Americans, though, as the British had six hundred dead or wounded compared to three hundred patriots.

The British credited Arnold with taking the battle to them rather than waiting in a defensive position as Burgoyne had expected. Gates was quite content with the day's results. His position was now secure, while Burgoyne was weaker and surely would have to retreat back to Canada.

Burgoyne expected to receive help from General William Howe coming up from New York. Little did he realize that Howe felt he had bigger fish to fry. He was moving his troops toward the American capital in Philadelphia. Burgoyne was on his own.

* * *

The Battle of Freeman's Farm was eclipsed in intensity only by the constant battle between Gates and Arnold. It may have been that Gates was concerned that Arnold's ferocious style would cause the Americans to lose the fight. Even worse was the possibility that Arnold's ferocious style might win the day as well as the glory Gates felt was his due. Gates replaced Arnold with Benjamin Lincoln, who had been promoted before Arnold and held seniority over him. The war of words between Arnold and Gates escalated, and Arnold asked for a pass to return to Washington's command. Gates called his bluff by giving him the pass. Arnold could not leave. He sensed that the battle in Saratoga could be the turning point of the war if only Gates would get out of the way.

October 7, 1777

The Americans now outnumbered the British ten thousand to six thousand. Burgoyne decided to attack believing that his trained regulars could take the field and the volunteer Patriot army would fold. They erected two battlefield forts called redoubts on either end of their lines. The Redcoats then advanced. Gates sent a small force with Daniel Morgan and Henry Dearborn as officers to meet the British column.

Arnold had been sent to his tent like an unruly schoolboy sent to the principal's office. He could see Morgan and Dearborn advance. He considered them his men going into battle. It was more than he could tolerate.

"No one will keep me in my tent today," he said as he leapt upon his black stallion. "Victory is ours, or death." He charged on toward the battlefield. The soldiers roared their approval when they saw their brave general advancing to the fray. Arnold rode about the field as a man possessed. This rugged terrain fighting was what he preferred. He would surely have been shot except he was continually moving.

The British pulled back to their defensive position with the redoubts on either end. The Patriots would have to capture one of these redoubts in order to flank the British defense. Arnold threw caution to the wind by racing between the firing lines to get to the weaker fortification. He called to his men there. As they attacked, Arnold was shot in the left leg, and his horse buckled beneath him. He was pinned to the ground. His men, inspired by his daring, rushed forward to take possession of the redoubt thus flanking the British.

A makeshift stretcher was made to carry Arnold away. At this point, a rider arrived from Gates summoning Arnold from the field. Arnold spoke to Henry Dearborn saying, "My leg is wounded, but I rather it had been my heart."

*   *   *

The battle was over for Arnold. Burgoyne was unable to retreat to Canada and was forced to surrender his army of 5,791 Redcoats and their German mercenaries. News of the British defeat traveled quickly to Europe. The French would now officially join the war on America's side believing the British could be beaten. Gates received the glory and accolades from Congress. They printed a medal in Gates's honor as the hero of Saratoga. There was talk in Congress of replacing Washington as commander-in-chief with Horatio Gates. No mention was made in Gates's report of Arnold's part in the battle.

Benedict Arnold's leg wound would never completely heal. Greater damage had been inflicted on Arnold's pride. His personal war with Congress and other military leaders would rage until one day the true hero of the Northern campaign would cross a line to become the most disdained traitor and spy in American history.

5

Aunt Sadie's Parlor

Neither Gramps nor I could get the trunk open no matter what we tried. Duct tape and WD-40 were not the answer. I tried a bobby pin which I had read somewhere might pick a lock. Whoever wrote that was either a man or never owned a lock that needed picking. Rather than waste more time and energy on a process we knew nothing about, we made the trek to the address we had been given. We stood side by side on the porch and braced ourselves for the unknown.

"I think we are at the moment of truth now," said Gramps. As he reached out and pushed the button, we could hear the bell inside ring loud and clear. We waited a few moments and Gramps began to whistle a made-up tune. I reached out and pushed the bell again while Gramps continued to whistle. Then a speaker on the side of the door squawked and came to life.

"Stop that infernal racket and go away and leave me alone!" said an unmistakably irritated lady.

"We apologize for disturbing you, ma'am. We don't mean to interrupt your afternoon," said Gramps politely.

"Then don't! I am not interested in whatever you are selling, and I don't make donations through my door, so go away."

"We are not selling anything or asking for anything, ma'am. I am Joshua Webb, and I am here with my granddaughter Greta. We bought a trunk at auction that I am told belongs to you."

There was a long pause and the voice said, "Why didn't you say so in the first place? Push through the door and come in so I can set the record straight." The door buzzed and Gramps and I grimaced at each other and proceeded through the entryway. On the other side was a narrow hall that led to what in previous years would have been called a parlor. A small fire burned in the fireplace on the far side of the room. A sofa and loveseat were in front of it. Sitting in a wheelchair was the owner of the irritated disposition. She appeared to be in her eighties. A young girl was standing nearby. The wheelchair's occupant pressed a lever on the armrest of the chair, and it moved swiftly across the room to the fireplace. There she leaned forward and picked a piece of wood from the woodbox and cast it into the flames. Then the wheelchair spun around to face us.

Finally, the lady spoke. "Well, let me look at you so I can decide how much trouble you are going be." After a slight pause, the lady continued. "She seems innocent enough, and I suppose you are old enough to know how to behave."

I smiled and felt an instant liking for this woman. Gramps seemed to be trying to figure out how to converse with her without setting her off.

"As I was saying, ma'am, we bought a trunk at auction yesterday and have been informed that it is rightfully yours."

"Why that old thing! I have been cleaning out some old junk from the attic and had Marguerite here send it out to auction." The young girl dutifully nodded in agreement to this statement. "That trunk has been in my attic for years. I never could open it. Who told you it was mine anyway?"

"We had a visit from Earle and John Henry who told us —"

"Earle and John Henry! I might have known. Those boys are a couple of no-good scalawags. They'd sooner let a skunk loose in your parlor than give you the time of day. They got no business chasing after my things. They think I am about ready to die and leave them a fortune. Well, they are wrong on both counts. I ain't about to die, and I ain't about to leave them diddly-squat. Now you can keep that old trunk and whatever is in it."

"Would it be too much trouble to ask if you have a key to the trunk?" I spoke up.

"You can ask, girl, but it won't do you no good. I have had that trunk for nigh on to forty years and never had any way to open it. I know something is in it, but there's no way of telling what it is. I couldn't get it open and neither could Horace, my dead husband. Of course, he wasn't much good with tools nohow. Once he was trying to open it and got so frustrated he almost took a sledgehammer to it. I told him if he cracked it, I would give him a whack and then he seemed to lose interest in it. It has been in our attic ever since."

My curiosity was getting the best of me and I said, "Where did the trunk come from Mrs. Woodruff?"

"We first got that trunk when we helped Uncle Ebenezer clean out his old barn. That old place was getting ready to collapse if a squirrel had stepped on it. He wanted to move everything to the new barn he had built. That trunk had been in that ramshackle barn since before Herbert Hoover was president. Uncle Eb said

'Git it out of here' so we took it. Horace was always kind of a pack rat. We just forgot about it then."

Gramps asked, "Do you know who the initials *RT* stand for? That might help us know why your nephews are interested in the trunk."

"No, I don't know for sure. I had a cousin whose name was Ralph Taylor, but that was only about fifty years ago, so it could not have been him."

"What can you tell us about Earle and John Henry, Mrs. Woodruff? Why are they so interested in the trunk?"

"There really isn't much to tell. They are my nearest living relatives, but you wouldn't know it if I didn't fess up to it. I hadn't heard from them for about fifteen years — not so much as a card or a phone call. Then about six months ago they started calling and pestering me. About two weeks ago they mentioned the trunk. You could have scraped me off the floor with a spatula. What did they care about an old trunk? I figured if I got rid of it they would leave me alone again, so I got rid of it." Sadie waved her hand as if brushing the trunk away. "No, you keep that old thing and if you find any thing valuable in it, it's yours."

"Do you know if they have ever had any trouble with the law, Mrs. Woodruff?"

"Never mind that 'Mrs. Woodruff' stuff. Just call me Sadie. And you, my dear, may call me Aunt Sadie," she said turning to me. "I have decided that I like you two. I'm glad someone I like bought that trunk, and I hope there's something good in it for you. No, I don't think they have been in any trouble with the law, but it wouldn't surprise me."

"Thank you very much, Aunt Sadie," I said, joining the conversation. "I want to use it to keep my sports equipment in. I play tennis and lacrosse at school. I really love old things like the trunk, and I like you too, Aunt Sadie."

The old woman smiled richly at this. "Tennis? I tried to do that once. Spent all my time chasing the ball around, and that net seemed ten feet high. Of course, I was using a wheelchair without a battery so it didn't move very well. More power to you, though. I used to watch Rod Laver, Arthur Ashe, and Jimmy Connors play. Connors was really a brat, though, so he was hard to root for. Ashe was a real gentleman. Laver, of course, was the best of all. That's why they called him 'The Rocket.'"

"I like Roger Federer and Rafael Nadal, Aunt Sadie. Federer has won more Grand Slam titles than anyone," I added.

"I don't know them, dearie, but isn't there a lady tennis player you like?"

"Of course. I have started following Sloane Stephens. She won the U.S. Open this year."

Gramps spoke again saying, "We will get the trunk open somehow, and we will bring you anything that would be of interest to you or your family."

"I can't imagine anything in it that I would need. If you do find an old picture or something related to us, then I would like to see it. Marguerite will give you my telephone number in case you need it."

"That sounds great, Mrs.Woodruff, I mean Aunt Sadie. We will definitely call you and let you know what we find," I promised.

"Now you two better get going. I have other things to do today, and I am sure you must have, too. Come back and see me again if you have a mind to."

"If we come again would it be alright if I bake some cookies to bring with us?" I asked. "I mean, are cookies okay for you to eat?

"For goodness sakes, child. You have just hit on a weak spot of mine. I just love fresh-baked cookies. You bring the cookies and I will have Marguerite put some tea on for us. Now I do hope you come back again."

"Thank you, Mrs. Woodruff, oh, I mean Aunt Sadie. We will be looking forward to seeing you again," added Gramps.

We bid her goodbye and headed out the door. As we neared the Jeep, Marguerite caught up to us.

"Excuse me, Mr. Webb. I just wanted to add that I played a small part in this." The young girl acted very sheepish as she explained what had happened. "I let the nephews know about the trunk being removed. They had insisted that I let them know if anything happened concerning the trunk. I feel guilty about telling them, but I didn't have the strength to say no. I apologize if I caused a problem for you."

"Don't be alarmed, Marguerite. I don't think they will be any real trouble for you or Aunt Sadie. Their interest in the trunk is rather puzzling, though. The trunk was sitting in an attic for forty years and now they start asking questions about it."

"There's more, Mr. Webb. I am aware that the nephews are concerned about how Mrs. Woodruff manages her assets. She does have some assets with value."

"Oh? Is someone managing her assets right now?"

"Yes sir. She has a lawyer named Milton Larsen and an accountant named Simon Rogers. Mrs. Woodruff trusts them very much. It's just that the nephews seem to be getting more and more aggressive in their demands."

"Thank you for telling us, Marguerite. Yes, they can be quite aggressive and intimidating, but I do suggest you let Aunt Sadie know if they try to contact you again. If anyone can deal with Earle and John Henry, it's Aunt Sadie."

"Thank you, Mr. Webb. I do want to be loyal to Mrs. Woodruff. She has always treated me fairly. She is even paying for part of my college costs. She hired me to be a companion, and the college expense wasn't part of the arrangement. When she found out about what my needs were, she wanted to help me out. She comes across as being miserly, but in reality she is very generous."

"Thanks again, Marguerite. I definitely agree with Greta's earlier comment that we really like Aunt Sadie. She seems fascinating, and I am not surprised by her generosity to you and to us. May I ask if you are at liberty to tell us what condition puts her in the wheelchair?"

"Certainly, Mr. Webb. As I understand it, she had polio as a child and has been in a wheelchair most of her life. Her husband, Horace, was a vice president at the local Merchants and Tradesmen bank. They were both well-respected members of the community. He passed away almost twenty years ago."

"It's been a pleasure meeting you and Aunt Sadie, Marguerite. I hope we can keep in touch."

"Thank you, Mr. Webb. Mrs. Woodruff enjoys having visitors, so please come again."

On the way home, Gramps and I went over our visit and what Aunt Sadie had said. "She seems like a sweet person to me, Gramps, even though she is a bit feisty."

"I agree with your assessment, Greta. She is up in years but still as sharp as a tack. Her nephews have not been paying much attention to her until recently. You have to wonder if they are only interested in an inheritance. For some reason, they think the trunk has more value than meets the eye. Perhaps they just don't want Aunt Sadie to be giving anything away. It's a shame folks don't pay attention to their older relatives for better reasons."

"I would like to visit her again, if it is all right with you, Gramps."

"That suits me just fine, kiddo."

6

The Farmer Spy

As I explained to Greta, General Washington remained committed to the recapture of New York. There was no Central Intelligence Agency at that time, but Washington wanted an officer to be in charge of intelligence operations. His search for someone to administrate and organize the espionage efforts eventually settled on Nathan Hale's classmate and friend Benjamin Tallmadge.

It seems that a new era of military intelligence was being promoted. Tallmadge suggested a new concept. Instead of using military men to go behind enemy lines, he wanted to recruit civilians who already traveled into occupied territory. One civilian he had known since boyhood was Abraham Woodhull. He was a farmer by trade and at that time had been arrested by the colonial troops for smuggling.

August, 1778

Major Tallmadge looked across the table at his friend. "Abraham, we have known each other quite a long time. I am sorry we had to meet in these circumstances."

"Benjamin, I am much obliged to you for arranging my release. You know Father and Mother could not get along without my help on the farm. That is the main reason that I have been involved in this business of smuggling. Ever since those bloody British took over New York City it's been the devil to pay for regular trade. You know we can't survive on just getting the Continental dollars for our goods. We must have the British Sovereigns. That's the reason for the 'London Trade.' That's a fancy name for smuggling, if I have ever heard one."

"I understand how it goes. The Tories in the city can't live on just tea and imported silks either. They have to have your milk, cheese, and eggs. That makes your entry into the city relatively easy. You are free to come and go there, but returning to Long Island is not as simple, I take it."

"No, there are brigands on the road who will rob you of your last ha-penny. The Whig thieves call themselves Cowboys and steal from you in the name of independence. The Tory brigands are called Skinners and rob you in the name of the Crown. Now to have been arrested by the Continental Army was not what I expected. It is more than I can endure. I am a Whig not a Tory. It's a terrible feeling to be in the middle of all this and be threatened by both sides. There must be a way to bring an end to this madness."

"That is our earnest hope, Abraham."

The farmer continued. "That end must come with the freedoms that every British subject enjoys." Abraham stood up and began pacing. "I wish I could serve in the Continental Army as you do, Benjamin. You know I would do anything to serve General Washington and the colonies."

The major now looked very seriously at his friend. "I was hoping you felt that way, Abraham. You know our cause is just and holy. The Crown has never treated us as subjects but as lackeys and dogs. We were born as free men, but our voices have fallen on deaf ears. Today, Abraham, I am here to give you your own freedom, but also, to enlist you in the cause of freedom."

"What are you alluding to, Benjamin? I can't shoulder a rifle. I can't leave my aged parents to take care of the farm alone. They would starve within a few months. I must continue to run our business no matter what my sympathies may be."

"That is precisely what I would want you to do, Abraham — continue your business. You can do more for the cause of liberty than any soldier carrying a musket."

"I don't understand you, Benjamin. I am a simple fellow. You will have to spell it out for me. What do you mean?"

"Information, of course, my dear fellow, information. We need to know what is going on in the city. We need to know when troops arrive or begin to move about. We need to know when ships are preparing to sail and what is the size of the lobster-back armies. We need to have eyes and ears in order to prepare to face the king's troops."

"Are you suggesting that I become a spy? Good heavens, man! Do you know what that means? Do you know what the penalty is? They not only hang you but they confiscate your property. My aged parents would perish. Since my two brothers have died, I must shoulder the responsibility of their care. I cannot fail them. I must not have my neck stretched."

"Shhhh, not so loud, Abraham. Yes, I am well aware of the penalties. Nathan Hale was my good friend. We went to school together at Yale. The poor boy talked to the wrong people. He

also did not have a good cover story. You have the perfect cover already. You travel to the city several times per month. Your business is the perfect ruse."

For a few moments there was silence as Woodhull paused to absorb what was being said. He had known Tallmadge since boyhood as they both had grown up in the Setauket community. The games they had played together as boys had now been replaced by tasks of the most serious nature. He felt excitement, fear, and concern.

"Benjamin, no one really respects spies. They are simply mercenaries seeking yellow gold. I could never do that. I am not a mercenary. I cannot profit from the war while so many are starving."

The two men fell silent again as the gravity of their conversation gripped them. The previous year, 1777, had been referred to as the year of the hangman because so many had met their fate with a noose. Abraham Woodhull, his eyes bright with excitement, looked at his boyhood friend and said, "I'll do it on one condition."

"Name your terms, Abraham. I will do all in my power to meet them."

Woodhull smiled at this and said, "I believe you can indeed meet my terms, Benjamin. It's this simple. I won't get financial reward. I just want to be reimbursed for expenses that I incur."

There was another pause, and then Major Tallmadge put his hand out for his friend to shake. Instead, Woodhull embraced him. The risks were very great but the need was vital. Neither man fully understood how the conversation that had just taken place would change history. A new nation was to be founded on the flames burning in their hearts. Those flames were the flames of liberty.

*   *   *

White Plains, New York — Two Days later

"Go right in, Major. The General is expecting you." Lieutenant Colonel Alexander Hamilton waved Tallmadge into the army headquarters at White Plains, New York. General Washington continually moved his headquarters as momentum in the war shifted. Now he was the guest of Jacob Purdy.

"Thank you, Colonel Hamilton." Tallmadge had left Woodhull two days ago and rode hard to deliver his news. He quickly passed the entryway and stood at attention before his commanding officer and saluted. The general stood at six foot two inches and weighed about 190 pounds. His physical presence exuded an aura of strength. His hair was brown, and his eyes were a bluish gray.

"At ease, Major. I have been anxious to hear about your mission. We are in need of good news right now."

"Our man is agreeable, sir, and I believe he will be able to make the mission work. He regularly travels to the city on business, so his presence there will not seem suspicious."

"What is his name, Major? Who is he, and can he be trusted?" the general wanted to know.

"I think you will agree that it is better to keep his name known only to me. The fewer people who know the particulars the better."

The general smiled at this. He was the supreme commander, but he liked it when his junior officers could tell him when he might be wrong. It gave him more trust in their sincerity.

"Yes, of course, you are right on that account. How will we communicate with him?"

"I have known him since boyhood and have absolute faith in him. He will send us dispatches regularly written between the lines of a book or pamphlet. He will use coded words for which I will have a key."

"What if those dispatches are intercepted? The bearer will be forced to talk. What then?"

"Not even the bearer will know the name of our agent. What's more, there will be a veil over the communication so the Redcoats will be unable to detect that there is any information being passed along."

"What do you mean, Major? Why can't they see plain writing?"

"That's the beauty of the plan, sir. The communication will be in writing that no one can see."

"What the devil are you talking about, Tallmadge? If they can't see it, then how can we?"

"It's a special ink, sir. No one can see it unless a reagent is applied to it that makes it visible again. You, sir, will have the reagent and be the first to see the messages."

Washington paused to absorb this information and then said, "Outstanding, Major! Outstanding! I have heard rumors about that type of ink. In fact, it was being developed by a doctor in England, of course." Washington stroked his chin as he remembered what he had heard. "I believe it was John Jay's brother James who was working on it. So the good doctor has finished it at last, has he? He referred to it as 'sympathetic stain.' We shall call it that as well."

"Keep in mind, General, that there is just a small quantity of the stain available right now. We hope to get more before long."

"As with everything else, Major, we will make do with what we have. Now Tallmadge, we need to get down to what we need from your agent. I want to impress upon you the requirements of these missions. There have been times in the past when exaggerated or even false information has been given to us. We need to have reports that we can rely upon for their accuracy. Exaggerated information is worse than no information at all."

"Yes sir. I will impress upon our agent the need for accuracy. I think you will, in time, come to rely on our agent and the reports that he gives. He is an exacting man."

"We still need a name, Major — a code name we can refer to him as. How about Culpepper for a name? That's a county in Virginia."

"Let's shorten it, sir. How about Culper? Let's call him Samuel Culper."

"Excellent, Major! Samuel Culper it is. Now let's discuss the monetary aspect of the project. Spies usually require a good bit of silver for the risks they take. What does our man expect to profit from this?"

"Sir, our agent is only looking for reimbursement of his expenses. It will cost for him to keep a spare horse along the route and lodging for a few nights. He will also be making more trips than he ordinarily would. He is not a wealthy man and does not have the means to fund these excursions."

General Washington stared for a moment at his subordinate. "Major, I am at a loss for words. He actually is not seeking financial benefit but simply to be reimbursed for his expenses? He then is a true patriot. Someday when all this is behind us I would very much like to meet him."

"There is one stipulation, General."

"Oh, and what would that be?"

"He must be paid in British Sterling rather than Continental dollars."

"That may prove to be difficult, Major."

"Yes, General, but if our agent is to travel into the city and gain information, he can't very well be spending Continental dollars. It would arouse suspicion."

"Yes, of course. He will be paid in British Sterling then. If he brings the information we need, he will be worth his weight in gold. Major, you have brought a good bit of cheer to me today. This could be the beginning of a grand venture. We now have eyes and ears in the most strategic city on the continent. Good day to you, Major."

Tallmadge saluted his commanding officer and stepped from the tent leaving the general with his thoughts. There was much that needed to be done. The British Army was known to be the finest and best-equipped army in the world. Washington had at his disposal a force that was numerically smaller and often ill-equipped. The regular task of feeding his men was a constant challenge. What had been proven to his advantage was information. Knowledge of the countryside and where to position his troops was usually in his favor. If he could know what the British plans were, then he could be ready for them. To have a spy or multiple spies in New York was what he dared hope for.

Benjamin, he thought, I pray you have found me the right man for this task.

7

The Secrets Con

My birthday was still a few months away, but this ⌐ felt like a birthday. I always love opening presents and seeing what's inside. It was exciting to buy the box in the first place. We had outbid other people, and I felt like we had won a prize or something. Now I was going to find out what that prize was.

"I can't believe we are about to find out what's inside this thing, Gramps. Why didn't we just open it in Ralph's shop?" I wondered out loud. We set the box down in the middle of the dining room floor and stepped back.

"Perhaps you remember the box that was once opened by a lady named Pandora," was Gramps's thoughtful reply.

"I sure do. She opened a box filled with demonic spirits, and then she couldn't get them back in the box so the world suffered. I don't see the connection here, though."

Gramps pursed up his lips and said, "We don't know what's inside here. I don't think it will be demons, but it could be something that is personal or even embarrassing to Aunt Sadie or someone in her family. The fact that Earle and John Henry wanted it badly enough to burglarize this house means there may be something significant here. It's not that I don't trust Ralph the locksmith, but

etter to be discreet about the contents until we know
are. Do you want to do the honors now?"

d forward and lifted the now unlocked latch. The lid was
and heavier than I expected as I moved it up and then let out
soft whistle. "Pyyyeeeewwww," I said. "It smells like a box that
hasn't had fresh air in it for a long, long time."

Ignoring the aroma, we both leaned forward to get a closer look.
Across the length of the trunk was a tray divided into halves. On
one side lay some books and on the other side lay papers that were
yellow with age.

"It does have a foul smell to it, Greta, but we should have
expected that. Those papers on the right have all the appearance
of being very old. What have we here on the left?" Gramps
reached in and lifted two books from the yawning lid of the trunk.
"This looks like a Bible and another old book."

"Oh raspberries! I was hoping for some gold pirate doubloons or
a flintlock pistol or something amazing from history."

"While you were hoping for a pistol, I was expecting just some
old clothes." Gramps was holding the Bible and the other book
in his left hand. With his right he thumbed some of the pages to
examine them. "This Bible is indeed historical. It wasn't printed
this century." He handed the Bible to me while he looked at the
second book more closely. "This is incredible, Greta. This other
book appears to be a real find. Wow, unless I miss my guess, this
book is a copy of *Common Sense*."

"*Common Sense*? That rings a bell. I don't remember much about
it, though."

"*Common Sense* was a pamphlet written back in the 1770s by a man named Thomas Paine. It was said to have been fuel to the fire that led to the Revolutionary War and the freedoms you were born to. I wonder if the items in this trunk are from that same era. We shouldn't assume anything at this point, but the binding on both the Bible and the book definitely look older than what I am used to seeing."

"Oh look at these papers, Gramps! They look like letters, and they weren't written with a ballpoint pen, I can tell you that." I lifted the papers from the trunk and held them up.

"Let me see, kiddo. Yes, look at the handwriting. It is far better than what you see today. In times past people took great pride in their penmanship. Look! There's a date on that letter — August 22, 1781. My goodness, Greta, this may be even better than some gold doubloons. Now look at that one. It looks like a page from an old newspaper — *The Royal Gazette*. The font used and the paper itself indicate extreme age. Not only that, but one page may have been the whole paper."

"Let's Google *The Royal Gazette* and find out something. My computer is open on the table. Give me a minute to log in." My workstation whirred into action and a minute later I gave Gramps a puzzled look. "This doesn't make much sense, Gramps. The *Royal Gazette* looks like a paper for Bermuda. That can't be what this one was."

"No, it can't be. Here on the paper it says published by James Rivington, printer. Add the name 'Rivington' to your search and see what happens." The keyboard sounded out the subtle taps and we both waited for the computer hum to finish.

"Bingo, Gramps! *The Royal Gazette* was published between 1777 and 1783 by James Rivington. He was in the New York area. Now we are getting somewhere."

"Yes, the date on the letter, and Rivington's *Royal Gazette*, and the book of *Common Sense* all point to the time of the Revolutionary War. Read the Gazette out loud if you will, Greta."

"I would like to read the first article but some of the letters look very strange or out of place, Gramps."

"Here, let me see. Yes, some of the letters look like an *f* but I think they are actually an *s*. Let me try to read this to you."

The Rivington Gazette — February 25, 1783

ORDERS

Head-Quarters, New York,

Should there be any persons, at present within the lines, whose houses or lands have been withheld from them on account of offences or supposed offences against the Crown, they are desired to make their respective claims to the offices of police in New York, on Long Island, or on Staten Island, who will report to same to the Commander in Chief.

All persons without the lines, who have abandoned estates within, are desired to send their claims to the offices of police aforesaid, and all persons occupying estates within the above descriptions, are strictly enjoined to take due care thereof as they will be made answerable for any damage, waste, or destruction, that may henceforward be committed on the same. They will likewise permit any person authorized from either of the above mentioned offices, to visit the said estates and take Inventories of all effects thereunto belonging.

"It is signed by O.L. De Lancey. This is certainly not what I expected to find, kiddo. Do you know what this is all about?"

"I haven't a clue," I had to admit.

"Judging by the date and the mention of New York this looks like a warning from a British officer to British sympathizers who were currently residing in homes of people who were Patriots. They were to be evacuated to allow the original owners to repossess the property. This fellow De Lancey was warning them not to do destruction to the homes that they were having to leave. I had no idea that these exchanges had to take place, but it makes perfect sense. Do another search specifically on James Rivington and see what we get."

Once again my fingers moved and a new fact came to light. "Look at that. He was a publisher during the Revolutionary War. His paper was very pro-British, but after the war people began to speculate that he was a spy for George Washington and the Continental Army. He may have been part of the Culper spy ring. That's a new one on me, Gramps. Have you ever heard of the Culper spy ring?"

"No, but let's keep working Google to find out what we can," he said.

I put the Culper spy ring into the search engine and studied the results with Gramps looking over my shoulder.

"Ta daaaaahhhhhhhhh," I shouted. "The Culper spy ring was headed up by Benjamin Tallmadge and included Abraham Woodhull, Caleb Brewster, Anna Strong, Robert Townsend, and possibly a female agent usually referred to simply as Agent 355. Samuel Culper was a fictitious name used to hide the true identities of the spies. The ring operated out of Long Island in the New York City area. After the colonial army was forced to flee New York, the British were left to occupy it. The spies came from Setauket and Oyster Bay, New York. Tallmadge reported directly to General Washington and was the only one to know the names of the other spies. The penalty for being caught as a spy was hanging. Wow, shades of Nathan Hale."

"That's absolutely right, Greta. Hale was a young man who was caught and hung as a spy."

"Is he the one who said he was sorry he only had one life to give for his country?"

"You've got it right again, Greta. At least that was attributed to him, but some have doubted the accuracy of that statement. He was a young man who was caught as a spy early in the war and was hung by the British."

"I wish you would quit saying that, Gramps. It gives me goosebumps."

"Sorry, Greta, but it is an important part of our history. Do you know what this means?"

"Not really, but I am hoping you will fill me in."

"It means that this trunk and its history goes back a lot farther than Aunt Sadie or her Uncle Ebenezer. History has a wealth of information for us to learn from. This trunk captures some of the lives of people living more than two hundred years ago. There are no pictures here, but these items are like snapshots in the lives of real people who are no longer with us. It doesn't really answer why Earle and John Henry would break into our house for it, though. Let's see what's underneath the tray." We lifted the wooden tray from the trunk and set it aside on the floor, to reveal some clothing.

"No great surprise to find clothing in a trunk." Gramps held up the first garment and it looked like britches made of very coarse material. We continued to lift clothing out of the box and set them on top of the tray on the floor.

"I have never seen any clothes like those, Gramps. What do you make of it?"

"Well, if the dates on the letter and newspaper are to be believed, I can guess the style of these clothes is from the same time period — the late 1700s. Whenever you think about dating something like this, it makes sense to take everything into account."

"What do you mean, Gramps?"

"Let me put it this way, kiddo. If we found a model airplane in the trunk, then we would have to wonder whether all the items came from the time when model planes were accessible. Since all the items seem rather old, then they might all belong to the same time period as the dates on the letter and newspaper."

"That makes sense. So what do we do now, Gramps? Do we give the trunk back to Aunt Sadie? Do you think Earle and John Henry would break into her house to get it? Does it really seem valuable enough to break the law and risk going to jail for?"

"Whoa, slow down, kiddo. Those are all good questions, but there still seems to be more to this than meets the eye. I don't want to report back to Aunt Sadie and give her partial information. There's no need to stir her up before we know all we can about these contents. We can keep searching the Internet for answers, but I am starting to get an itch to make a trip. An Internet search can give us a lot of information, but nothing beats seeing for yourself."

"I'm with you, Gramps. Literally as well as figuratively."

"I'll take that as a vote of confidence, Greta. Let's find out what we can about Rivington and see if there is anyone we can go to and ask questions. I know a man who lives on Long Island who may be able to help fill in some blanks for us. He's a retired history professor. I think you would enjoy meeting him. Besides, his wife makes great Oriental food. I'll give him a call and see if we can set up a meeting. This may not be a treasure chest, but it is real and historical."

"I would say it is real, and historical, and a boatload of fun. I also do hereby proclaim this a mystery." I held up one hand for a high five. Gramps paused as if to think, and then he nodded agreement and we slapped hands.

8
The Merchant Spy

Greta and I were going to learn a lot about the Revolutionary War. In particular, we would find out about the spy ring that became essential to the retaking of New York. Abraham Woodhull was the first member of that ring, but more than one spy was needed to make the scheme work. Woodhull traveled to and from the city, but a necessary component was to have a man actually stationed inside the city, someone that Woodhull could trust with his life. He would find that man in someone he grew up with in Oyster Bay, Long Island.

*   *   *

On a cool evening in November 1778 two men walked along the path away from the house and listening ears. They glanced around in the direction of Oyster Bay and the waterway known as Long Island Sound.

"Father, are you unwell? You seem so listless today."

Samuel turned toward his son and said, "Would that it were only so, my poor boy. Of a truth I long for the days when my only concern was your well-being in your occupation in Manhattan." They spoke in hushed tones as they walked through the garden. "Do you see what they have done?" He pointed to the long rows of stumps where his once proud fruit trees had grown. "They did this o' purpose. This was once the finest orchard on Long Island, but look at it now. What do you see? They said the firewood was needed, but I know better. They did it to humble me. They did it to show their authority and absolute control."

The younger man began to ponder the situation his family found itself in. At what point does a person begin a secret life as a spy? For Robert Townsend, it was a gradual change over the course of the war. His father was a wealthy merchant who was also known to have a rebellious nature. Samuel was a Quaker but refused to abide by some of the principles that most Quakers held. He was also politically outspoken. During the French and Indian War, Samuel had been arrested by local authorities regarding a letter he had written protesting the treatment of prisoners. Samuel and Robert were both Patriots, when the British invaded and took control of Long Island.

Robert had been involved in the Battle of Brooklyn for the colonists. He could not say he had actually fought in it. Because of his Quaker convictions he doubted that he could fire a musket at another man. After his father had been arrested, both he and Robert were forced to swear allegiance to the Crown. That seemed to quiet the Townsend zeal for independence, but it did not extinguish it. While Robert worked as a merchant in Manhattan, the British occupied Long Island. A group of soldiers led by Lieutenant Colonel John Simcoe took up residence at the Townsend family home. Throughout the colonies the British had inflicted damages to properties and humiliations on the residents. John Simcoe was one of the worst of the perpetrators.

The Townsend family suffered many indignities during this occupation. They were relegated to live in a small portion of their home. The British cut down Samuel's prize orchard to use for firewood. The greatest offense of all, however, was when Simcoe openly flirted with Robert's sister. He had even given her a card expressing his affection for her. How could an oath taken under duress be considered binding in the face of such indignations?

While working in Manhattan, Robert began to observe the movements of the occupation troops. He overheard conversations and could sense when a military action was in the air. If only Washington could hear what he heard and see what he saw. If only Washington could know what he knew.

As a Quaker, Robert could not join the Continental Army, but surely there must be something he could do. His brother Solomon had been helping the Patriot cause by smuggling provisions to the colonists. But what could he do to help? He was more of a bookkeeper than a warrior. But how could he just stand by while Colonel Simcoe flirted with his sister? What dangers could she be in from these lobster-backed soldiers who occupied their town as well as their very house? Even more disheartening was seeing how subdued his father had become. His father had always been brave and stood up for a cause that he believed in. Now he spoke only in quiet tones within his own house. He was afraid. He knew of the British prison ships, where colonists who had been seized were held and had their loyalties questioned. Samuel was fearful of being sent to one of these ships and never returning.

What should a true Quaker do in these circumstances? Politics was not something a good Quaker is called to take sides on. The leaders of his church promoted pacifism and remained neutral during this conflict. The more he heard this, the more he began to doubt the teaching of his church. It seemed as though neutrality was in reality siding with the Crown against the rebels. As these thoughts kept coming to Robert, his attitude began to take a new direction, and he began to listen to a new voice. Thomas Paine was also a Quaker, and he had written very persuasively about what he believed the true Quaker position should be. Paine's writings were called Common Sense. They were published as a pamphlet and then openly discussed by the colonists in taverns and homes across the land. The Quaker leaders condemned Paine's writings, but his voice continued to be heard.

Robert began to mull over what he had heard recently of the *Common Sense* pamphlet. "A government of our own is our natural right." Men had been debating the issue of independence for several years now. The pamphlet had been printed in newspapers and discussed everywhere that the colonists had the freedom to speak up. Robert was a fourth-generation colonist. He had grown up hearing about the monarchs of the mother country. Now Paine wrote, "Did the monarchy ensure a race of good and wise men it would have the seal of divine authority, but as it opens a door to the *foolish*, the *wicked*, and the *improper*, it hath in it the nature of oppression." Now Robert saw the oppression of the monarchy. He could feel it in his own home. His own dear father was clearly oppressed in spirit by this monarchy.

Quakers held to the doctrine of pacifism. A Quaker should never bear arms in a conflict or even take political sides. But didn't his religious leaders take the side of the Crown by telling all not to oppose the British authorities? How could he reconcile the situation? When he said his prayers, he yearned for God to show him the right course of action. Which authority should be obeyed? Should he obey the Crown and his church leaders or the direction his heart was now leading him? Did he have the courage to take a stand in the face of injustice? He was not brave like his brother Solomon. He was the quiet one of the family.

Perhaps he just needed a new diversion. A new business venture had presented itself to him recently. There was a coffeehouse near his present employment that he could invest in. His bookkeeping position left him with some time on his hands in the city, and he could use that time wisely by additional employment. It was also a way to begin a new chapter in his life. He was not an outgoing person, and Father had suggested he get around town more and meet new people. His brothers were more adept at being social than he, but perhaps he could follow their example. Perhaps he could learn something new, and even something useful.

"Halt! Who goes there?" a voice called out.

"Are ye blind, Corporal? Can ye not see that it is Samuel Townsend who is the master of this house?"

"Meaning no disrespect, sir, but you are master of this house only by King George's grace and by Colonel Simcoe's pleasure. Now you know that curfew is drawing nigh and you should be inside. Shall I escort you there, sir?"

"I do believe that my son and I can find the path from the stumps in my orchard to the house without your assistance. Now by your leave we shall go there directly."

"As you will, sir," the sentry stepped aside.

Father and son moved back up the path toward the house. "So you see, my boy. We are here at the pleasure of the good Colonel Simcoe. Did he build this house with his own two hands? Did his grandfather come to this shore in the last century? If he had planted the fruit trees he would not have so readily cut them down."

"We must be patient, Father. Perhaps God will be merciful to us and remove these Redcoats. The colonists can win this battle as they did in Saratoga. I do admire men such as Benedict Arnold. The good General Arnold almost lost his leg, but his heroism in the field won the day. Father, do you realize the British general Burgoyne surrendered over five thousand men after the battle of Saratoga?"

"Ah yes, my boy. The memory warms my heart, but that was a year ago. Back then I was master in my own home. I was never told to go inside before curfew. The British control Long Island, and my poor fruit trees are no more. Saratoga is but a distant memory now."

"That is not the end of the story, Father. I hear things in the city that I believe are very encouraging."

"What things do you hear, my son? Tell me the news that will bring light to these dull eyes of mine."

"Only this, Father, which may be depended upon. Because of Saratoga, other world powers may be inclined to aid the American cause."

"Really? Do you mean France will come to our aid? I had thought they would have had quite enough of fighting the British."

"On the contrary, Father, the French and English continue to be at odds with one another. The French have now pledged to come to our aid."

"That is only a rumor, Robert. Don't believe everything you hear, my son."

"Nay, Father, it is true. I have heard it from the English officers themselves. Benjamin Franklin has been in France to further our cause and win the favor of King Louis XVI since the hostilities began. Now an alliance has been signed. The British speak of it. They say it with disdain and bravado. They believe they can vanquish the French as well as the colonial army. So you see, Father, we have good reason to hope."

"Ah, that is my prayer, Robert, but in my spirit I begin to lose heart that it will happen in my lifetime. I do have hope for you, though, my boy."

"We must never lose hope, Father. New fruit trees can be planted. Colonel Simcoe will not stay forever. What's more, my sister only tolerates his attention so he will be kinder to you."

"The only kindness I wish from the colonel is his hasty departure."

"Oh, Father, I would that it were in my power to make that happen!"

"Don't trouble yourself, dear boy. Don't trouble yourself." The older man put his arm on his son's shoulder and the two walked slowly toward the house. Young Robert Townsend did trouble himself, though. He did more than trouble himself. He began to ponder a course of action.

9
The Newspaper Article

Mom and Dad were enjoying their trip to the UK, but I wasn't feeling left out. They were faithful in sending post cards and calling me. They had spent time in London and were now driving around Wales and Scotland. They said they enjoyed the English countryside even more than the city sights.

For my part, I was having the time of my life. Staying with Gramps was like a vacation. Gramps and I could go play tennis and I could catch up on my reading. Even so, the mystery box had given this vacation an added touch. It made a friend for me with Aunt Sadie and I hoped to see more of her.

"Those shishkabobs smell great, Gramps. I love it when you barbecue. I think I like the colors almost as much as the smells. Green peppers, cherry tomatoes, onions and chicken makes for a perfect skewer."

"Your praise makes it all worthwhile, Greta. Gram is a fabulous cook, but while she's gone we don't have to starve."

After dinner Gramps and I went through the contents of the trunk I bought at auction. I am not sure what I expected. I have gone through old things in trunks before and usually it is material that quickly finds its way to the ragbag. This was really different. There were books and letters and what appeared to be clippings from a newspaper. We sorted through the trunk and began to arrange the contents on the floor with the paper items on the table nearby.

The lower portion of the box contained a moth-eaten blanket and a three-cornered hat that Gramps greatly admired. There was also a somewhat full set of men's clothing. There was a blue coat that must have come down to a man's knees. Two long sleeved linen shirts, a pair of breeches, two pair of gray knee high stockings, and a pair of black leather shoes with metal buckles were unfolded and set aside. I let out a big laugh when I pulled out a man's wig. It was gray and must have rested from the top of the owner's head down to the shoulders. I tried to get Gramps to try it on, but he wanted no part of that. I put it on myself and went to look for a mirror to get the full effect.

"It's too bad men don't still wear these," I teased.

Gramps replied, "Men do try to cover their heads with a hairpiece today. They just make every effort to make it look like the original hair so it won't be noticed as much. Since Gram likes me the way I am, I don't see the need."

"Yes, but you sure do like to wear hats, Gramps."

"I certainly do. Is that a problem?"

It was obviously time to change tactics. "Not at all, and I like you the way you are, too. Even if you won't model the wig for me."

We turned our attention to the items from the upper portion of the box that we had set aside earlier. Sprawled out on the table were letters, some old paper that looked like blank stationery, several news clippings from the *Royal Gazette*, an old book, a Bible, and a journal.

"Look at the dates on the letters, Gramps. They are from 1778 and appear to be written between sweethearts."

Gramps let out a soft whistle and said, "Well kiddo, it sounds like shades of Romeo and Juliet."

I gave him a wry smile and then added, "Gramps! Look at this newspaper. It's another page from the *Royal Gazette*. It looks like an ad for migrants to come up north to Nova Scotia."

"Read it to me, kiddo."

"I am not sure I can make out all of the words. Can you read it?"

"Let me see. Wait, let me get my reading glasses on." Gramps retrieved his glasses from his pocket. "Ah, it looks like the same old English font we saw before. Yes, it is from Rivington's newspaper all right," he said while scanning the paper. "Just remember these letters look like an *F* but I think they are actually an *S*. With that in mind we can make sense out of them. Listen to this."

"To those Loyal Refugees who either have already left, or who hereafter may leave their respective countries in search of other habitations.

We the subscribers, your countrymen and fellow-sufferers hearing that several families have already arrived in Nova-Scotia from New York, and that many others intend coming to some of these Northern Colonies next Spring, think it our duty to point out this island to you, as the most eligible country for you to repair to, of any we know between this and New-Jersey. The SOIL is good. It is well wooded and free from rocks. The climate so good that Fevers and Agues are unknown. Water everywhere excellent. The harbors are spacious, numerous and safe. The rivers, bays, lakes, and coasts abounding with a great variety of shell and almost all other sorts of fish, and good of their kinds. The government is mild. But very few Taxes, — these very light, and raised solely for the benefit of the island. There is room for tens of thousands and land in the finest situations on harbors, navigable-rivers, and bays to be had exceedingly reasonable. Cattle are plenty — witness the droves which have been this year taken to Halifax Market."

Here Gramps paused to give his opinion. "This is really something else, Greta. We can forgive the mistake of calling Nova Scotia an island. It is really a peninsula. This seems to be a newspaper ad appealing to British Loyalists to come to Nova Scotia. This may have been at the end of the Revolutionary War when the Loyalists felt they were at risk by Patriots who would move in and do them harm. It goes on."

"Before we came here we were told as perhaps you may be the worst things possible of the country such as that the people were starving. We should get nothing to eat and should ourselves be eaten up by insects. And much more equally groundless. We have found the reverse too true. Therefore do not attend to such reports, but come and see and depend on the evidence of your own senses."

"It is signed by officers of the King's Rangers. What do you think of that, Greta?"

"It sounds like they had mosquitoes back then just like today." I couldn't help but laugh at my own joke while Gramps smiled at me.

"Be serious, kiddo. This shows us not all people living in America wanted to be a part of the new country of the United States.

Many felt like they had to leave because they had supported the king and the Redcoats during the war."

"You're right, Gramps, and I never realized that before. I always pictured us winning the war and just British soldiers and perhaps their families going back to England. It also seems like a hard sell."

"What do you mean kiddo?"

"Well, it's like England didn't want a flood of people coming back to England so they put these men up to writing glowing reports to entice folks to go somewhere else."

"You are probably right about that sweetheart." Gramps paused there for reflection. "I can't see Earle and John Henry wanting to burglarize our home to get this clipping, but to me it is an incredible find. I am not sure what Aunt Sadie's heritage is but she might be very interested in this."

"She might have ancestors who had to leave to avoid persecution, or maybe they were Patriots who wanted to move into houses that were occupied by Tories."

"That's right, Greta. Whoever kept this clipping in the trunk didn't put it there for us to find. They put it there because the area was in a transition at the end of the war."

"It must have been exciting to live during those times, Gramps. Sometimes I daydream about what it would have been like to live in times like that. What adventures they must have had."

"Adventure sounds like a lot of fun, Greta, but I imagine that there were some dull times, too. There was also the little problem of putting food on the table to feed a hungry family. The local market did not have all the items we enjoy — if there was a local market."

"Hmm, you're right, Gramps. How about all the dangers they faced from the Indians? I read the *Last of the Mohicans* by James Fenimore Cooper and times were brutal back then."

"There were Indian wars, of course, but there were also times when settlers and Native American Indians lived peaceably and helped one another." I could tell that Gramps wanted to give a fair picture of early America.

"Yes, I remember how Squanto came and helped the pilgrims and taught them how to fish and raise crops to feed themselves. That was pretty amazing since he himself had been kidnapped by foreigners and taken to Europe."

"If it's adventure you want though, I believe we may have some adventures ahead of us. I think we should take that trip, kiddo."

"Where to, Gramps?"

"How about New York City and its surrounding burroughs?"

"I could be talked into that. I have never been to New York City. Can we see a Broadway play while we are there? That would be slick."

"We won't find anything to research at a play right now. We need to be focused on finding out more about Rivington and the Culper spy ring, and why this box seems to be important to Aunt Sadie's nephews. I won't say no to a play just yet, but let's say it's doubtful."

"Do you think a trip to New York will help solve the mystery of why Earle and John Henry want the box?"

"Our best clues right now are the pages from the *Royal Gazette*. That points to the New York area during the time of the Revolution. Then there's the old books and the letters. I only glanced over the letters since I felt like I was reading someone else's mail. One of the books looks like a journal or a ledger of some business transactions."

"You can have the books, Gramps. I am interested in the letters. I don't think anyone dead for more than a hundred years will mind if I read them."

"No, I don't imagine they would. Still, this *Gazette* article is a real eye-opener. It shows that America was really a mixed bag. There were the Loyalists, or Tories who did not want to rebel against the Crown. They were on the losing end of the war, though, and had to leave or face retribution."

"What about the books, Gramps? Did you find any clues in the Bible or *Common Sense* or the journal?"

"Yes, the journal has a number of entries, and the bottom of each page is initialed with 'RT.' It looks like 'RT' was the owner of the trunk and not its maker."

"What else in the trunk is important, Gramps?"

"We have to think that everything in the trunk is important, Greta. The clothes show us the character of the owner, or perhaps his position in society. He wasn't a frontiersman like Daniel Boone. He was probably a merchant or a shopkeeper. He kept a journal of business transactions. He was paying attention to what happened to the Loyalists after the war. He may have sympathized with them or he may have celebrated that they were leaving. His initials were RT as shown on the trunk and in the ledger. The Bible indicates that he was a religious man. Bibles were not as easy to come by then. The book *Common Sense* suggests that his political persuasion was on the Patriot side of the war. We may learn more about him personally from the letters in the trunk. That being said, I am repeating my suggestion that we take a field trip. Your folks are on a trip to England. Surely we can travel to New York City."

"This trunk is making me see the Revolutionary War days in a whole new light," I admitted. "It isn't just words in a history book. I can see how real people went through the war and either came out on top or suffered. I think your field trip idea is Phi Beta Kappa. When do we leave?"

10

Culper Sr. Faces His Fears

When Greta and I went through the trunk, we were surprised by what we found. Rivington's paper pointed us to the New York City area. I had always thought of Boston and Philadelphia as being important during the Revolution, and indeed they were. I just didn't realize that the New York City area was very prominent. Actually, the events that took place around New York City were pivotal to the war. Long Island was under British control, but many Patriot sympathizers lived there. None played a bigger role for the Patriot cause than a humble farmer named Abraham Woodhull.

*   *   *

Abraham sat at his writing table with his goose quill in hand. His thoughts turned back to the last several months as he replayed the images in his mind. At one time he had seemed destined for a simple life as a farmer. He enjoyed the work and had no real interest in the study of books. As the third son, his education was merely an afterthought. Then both of his brothers passed away, and he was now due to inherit the farm with its responsibilities. He had to care for his aging parents. He was thankful that he had no wife or responsibilities other than them. Then again, there was Mary Smith. She was a near neighbor and, Abraham sighed, interested him very much. He knew he could learn to care for her if he were free. He was not free now, though. He was a spy, and he knew that if he were ever caught he would receive a spy's reward at the end of a rope. His property would be confiscated, and his parents or wife would be left destitute. How could he ever hope to wed with turmoil swirling around.

Still, it was his duty to serve his country. Benjamin Tallmadge had long been his friend, and General Washington had his utmost respect as the finest man he had ever known. Someday he hoped to meet the general. He had even dreamed of walking into the general's headquarters and saluting that great man. The general would then reach out a hand to shake his as a gesture of respect. It was just a dream. He knew the general by reputation only.

Abraham knew his reports were well received. Major Tallmadge had assured him that Washington read them with a careful eye. He had put a great deal into these reports, meticulously crafting them so as not to communicate any distortion of the facts. He prided himself on accuracy and detail. It was this attention to detail that had begun to worry him. When he spoke to folks and asked questions about military activity, he could almost feel eyes staring at him. He was intent on keeping his identity as a spy a secret from the townspeople. Traveling into the city as often as he did must surely give rise to suspicion, but he took every precaution. He had the perfect cover for this business. He was a farmer who went to town to sell his goods or trade his produce. The Patriots turned a blind eye to selling goods to the British. Every farmer did it. The British wanted his butter and cheese and meats and were willing to pay for it in British Sterling silver. His expenses were transacted with the same coinage. Colonial dollars could not be used in New York City. It would arouse too much suspicion. Colonial dollars did not purchase much anywhere. British silver was needed to buy seed for planting or feed for farm animals.

Now, he had become increasingly depressed regarding the whole situation. He had spoken of his concerns to Tallmadge, who had traveled to his home to talk with him. Although he liked seeing his friend, having him visit was most unnerving. Tallmadge was very recognizable, and everyone knew he was in charge of Patriot intelligence. If anyone saw him, visiting Woodhull the game would be over. Tallmadge was even now hiding in the woods nearby.

That was not his only trouble. In a room down the hall were two British officers. They had come unexpectedly to his home and demanded lodging. Their request was not unusual in these dangerous times, but why did they have to come here? Why now? Were they lying in wait to take him prisoner? They did not act suspicious but simply disdainful of all colonists. Abraham knew that the actions of the British were causing many colonists to switch loyalties to the Patriot cause. Many people now derogatorily called them lobster-backs who a year ago had favored remaining with the Crown. Abraham hoped his "guests" would not stay long. He prayed they would not catch wind of Tallmadge's visit.

Woodhull stretched his hand out to dip the goose quill into the bottle of fluid again. That bottle itself gave him some comfort in the work he was doing. It wasn't really ink in the bottle. It contained a fluid that remained invisible to the naked eye until a reagent was applied. Only Washington possessed the reagent. He would write his report, and no one would be able to read it but Washington. This time, Woodhull would give the report to Tallmadge himself who would transport it to headquarters.

This was a bit unusual. In the normal course of events, he would be at his brother-in-law Amos Underhill's boardinghouse in Manhattan. He would give a report to Austin Roe, who would travel to Setauket and make a drop where it would be picked up by Caleb Brewster.

Ah, good old Caleb. What a brave soul he was. He had the spirit of Blackbeard the pirate. He was also involved in the black market, but who wasn't during these times? Caleb would take the packet, then cross the Long Island Sound in his whaleboat. He would either give the report to Tallmadge or ride himself to Washington's camp.

Every one knows that Caleb is in this business. It's no secret, but only a few know about me, thought Abraham. Only Tallmadge and Brewster and Roe know about me. I trust God that no one else knows.

Suddenly, the door burst open and two figures rushed into the room. Abraham jumped to his feet knocking over his precious ink supply. He fairly screamed thinking his worst fears had come true. Then the two figures started laughing with delight. They were his two nieces, Abby and Sophie. They had barged in planning to cheer up their poor uncle. He had been looking so dejected lately, so they took it upon themselves to change that.

"Oh Uncle, you looked so dreary at dinner tonight that we wanted to cheer you up a bit. You should have seen the look on your face just now," Abby exclaimed.

Poor Abraham finally managed to compose himself. "Ah girls, you gave me such a fright. Look, I have spilled my ink bottle." All three looked at the paper on the desk with the bottle lying on its side. Woodhull had a look of apprehension while the girls just looked relieved.

"You have no cause for alarm, uncle," Sophie observed. "Your ink bottle seems empty and no ink stain is on the paper." Woodhull picked up the bottle and the paper nervously.

"Yes, it looks like I am out of ink, girls."

"It's a wonder the paper is blank, Uncle Abraham. We thought you had written a book by the length of time you were up here," Abby said.

Woodhull arranged his desk as best he could and then looked at the girls in a serious manner. "Now girls, you must leave me to my work. I have much to do." He patted them on the shoulders as he ushered them out the door.

The girls left with a feeling of satisfaction that their mission was accomplished. They had cheered their dear uncle up. Abraham was anything but cheered up, though. He collapsed into his chair hoping the British soldiers would not realize what had taken place. On top of everything else a bottle of the precious liquid had been spilled. To Abraham this ink was more valuable than gold. It provided that extra layer of security so necessary to his safety and peace of mind. What's more was that his pages were indeed ruined. The stain had dashed about the pages, and there was no way for him to tell if his report was intelligible or not. He could not send it to General Washington now.

Late that night, Woodhull crept down the hall to the front door. He had purposely oiled its hinges to make this trip with the least possible noise. Once outside, he paused for several minutes and then proceeded around the back of the house and into the woods. These were his woods, but the dreariness of the night and the fear of getting caught added to his uneasiness. About a mile away from the house he came to a footpath and began to follow it. He traversed another mile and slowed his pace. Up ahead he saw the old willow tree he was searching for.

"Benjamin," he called out in little more than a hoarse whisper.

"Over here," came a soft reply. "Did you bring anything I might eat?"

"Yes, of course." The two wasted little time in small talk. "Here is a bit of bread and a flask of water. Benjamin, my nerves have been shattered. There are two Redcoats staying at my house." Woodhull went on to describe the trick his nieces had played on him and the spilled bottle of fluid.

"It was a disaster, Benjamin. If I had possession of a pistol, I would mistakenly have shot one of them, and where would I be now?" In the darkness Woodhull could not see the smile on his friend's face.

"Did you finish the dispatch Abraham?"

"Yes, here it is. But Benjamin, I don't know if I can continue this. I live in fear every day."

"General Washington examines your reports very carefully. You are his most trusted agent."

Now it was Woodhull's turn to smile. To have the respect of the general he so admired made him believe the risk was worth it.

*   *   *

Woodhull was feeling a lot of pressure on himself. A few days later an event took place that made the vise even tighter. A man named John Wolsey was questioned by the British and named Woodhull as a person who may be involved in espionage for the colonists. What made Wolsey suspect Woodhull was never discovered. He may have been a visitor to Roe's tavern and heard a side remark, or he may have noticed Woodhull traveling to Manhattan on frequent occasions.

Whatever the reason, the news was passed on to Colonel John Simcoe of the Queen's Rangers. Simcoe was in Oyster Bay at the time but rushed to Setauket to arrest Woodhull. He and a squad of Rangers pounded on the door of the Woodhull homestead to demand Abraham's surrender. His father, Richard, came to the door and pleaded that his son was not at home. A thorough search proved him right, but Simcoe would not be turned away empty-handed. He unsympathetically ordered the elder Woodhull to be beaten.

Abraham returned days later to be greeted with this disquieting news. How could he stay at home now fearing that Simcoe would return? How could he continue with this business and be of service to General Washington and the Patriot cause? He wanted to retire to a quiet life without fearing the sound of marching boots or hoofbeats on the road.

He communicated to Tallmadge that his days as a spy were coming to an end. He didn't want to shirk his duties and leave the general empty-handed. He still believed that the service he rendered had value. He had an idea. Perhaps he could recruit a replacement to continue the work. He had someone in mind.

He had on occasion been meeting a man at the boardinghouse of Amos Underhill. That man lived and worked in New York City. He had known that man for many years and knew he could trust him to protect a confidence. If that man would agree to help then the Culper spy ring would be complete.

11
Road Hazards

I always loved making field trips and it wasn't my first outing with Gramps. He and Gram often came with our family to visit people, and sometimes we went on vacations together. On this trip I was feeling like he was a detective, and I was his partner. I thought about calling him Mr. Holmes and having him call me Watson. That would have been silly though.

"Maybe one of these days we can take a trip, and I will do the driving." I peered over at Gramps to get his reaction.

"That day will surely come sweetheart, but it won't be until you get your learner's permit. Did I tell you about when I taught your Aunt Becky how to drive?"

"Only about a hundred times, but I don't mind hearing it again."

"Nope, you had your chance. I refuse to make it a hundred and one. Let's stop at this gas station. You probably need to go potty."

"Who are you kidding, Gramps? You need to go more often than I do. I will check out the candy counter."

Gramps pulled into the station and up to the gas pump. "Don't get anything your parents will blame me for. While you are at it, though, get me a small coffee with cream only. Here's five bucks."

"You can trust me. Scout's honor." I said this with three fingers on my hand pointing to the sky. Gramps set the nozzle on to pump the gas, then went to wash the windows. Inside the store I was checking out some packaged pastries when I noticed a man at the end of the aisle. He was wearing a dark brown suit and sunglasses, which I thought was odd. It was an overcast day and the man was mistaken if he thought the sunglasses made him look cool. What was more interesting was that the man was holding a magazine, but I didn't think he was actually reading it. I began to wonder if he was looking at me from behind those sunglasses. Shaking my head as if to get the cob webs out I edged toward the door. Once outside I made a beeline to where Gramps was finishing up. I hopped in the shotgun position and we started off down the road.

"What? No snack?" Gramps gave me a puzzled look.

"No, I don't really need anything right now. Here's your five bucks back."

"I appreciate the return, but you didn't get my coffee either."

"Oh, I'm sorry. I forgot all about it."

"Well, it's no biggie, I guess. Your mind just seems to be wandering a little. Is there anything wrong?"

"Actually, it's very strange. There was a man in the shop who just gave me the willies."

"Really? What did he look like?" Gramps threw me a look of concern.

"He was wearing a brown suit and had on sunglasses, which I thought was out of place in this cloud cover. He was going bald and very pale, so he didn't look like he spent much time out of doors. Did you see him?"

"Yes I did. He drove up in a dark SUV and parked without getting gas. Then he went inside, but that doesn't seem too unusual. Also, don't say *bald* like it's a disease. You know I am sensitive about that."

"Sorry, Gramps, but inside he just picked up a magazine and acted like he was reading it."

"What do you mean by *acted*?"

"There are two reasons I think he was only acting like he was reading. One is it was *Bride* magazine, and two is he had it open but never turned the page."

"I have to agree that sounds peculiar. Maybe he has a daughter who is getting married soon."

"If that were the case, his daughter would have enough *Bride* magazines to sink a ship. Nobody has to pick them up at a gas station in the middle of nowhere. It made me feel like he was watching me, and after Earle and John Henry breaking in, I think it makes sense to be a little suspicious."

"I don't disagree with you there. Let's not get paranoid about this, though. We don't want to be jumping at shadows. This world does have some strange people doing strange things, and I forgive you for not getting my coffee."

I looked up to catch his smile. Gramps had a great sense of humor and I enjoyed his company very much. My parents are tops, but they feel their responsibility and have to discipline me. Gramps could just take things in stride and enjoy our time together. It was even fun to be teased by him.

"Oh look!" I said. "That sign is advertising the county fair. Can we go?"

"We can't stop and see it now. Steve and Eileen are expecting us for dinner in Queens. We might be able to catch it on our way back if we have time to spare."

"What's our itinerary then, captain? Is it batten down the hatches? Full speed ahead and don't spare the octane?" I don't have a clue as to what octane is, but Gramps uses the phrase, so I assume it makes sense.

"We shall spend the evening with Steve and Eileen Kim. You remember I mentioned them. Steve is a retired professor of American history. I believe he can give us some information on this James Rivington fellow."

"Couldn't we have just called him and gotten the information over the phone?"

"Yes, that's true, but I haven't seen Steve in several years so I want to see them in person. Sometimes you can find out a lot more by talking to someone in person than just having a phone conversation. I called ahead, and he seemed anxious to have some visitors. Besides, I think you will really enjoy the interview with them. Then we may go to Oyster Bay and Setauket."

"That's right. That's where members of the Culper spy ring spent time. It's hard to imagine that George Washington paid spies out of his own pocket. I never knew he did anything but fight battles and become president."

"Washington had many irons in the fire, kiddo. He had to worry about keeping his army together. He had men with short-term enlistments, and when the going got tough some left, and some even deserted. He had to worry about food, ammunition, and fuel to keep the men warm."

"Right, I have heard a lot about the cold winter of Valley Forge."

"Yes, but most people don't realize that Washington had other problems as well. He had to negotiate with the Continental Congress about many things. In some ways, Washington was quite a public relations man. When they won battles like Trenton and Princeton things seemed easy, but when they lost, he had to bolster the public as well as the troops. He was diplomatic in dealing with the population to keep them on the side of the revolutionaries. Things were not easy for Congress, either. Financing a revolution was not a simple thing for a group of independent colonies. They couldn't tax like today's government. There was no income tax or federal tax. Don't get me started on that subject, though. I would bore you the rest of the afternoon complaining about taxes."

Analyzing these new ideas was starting to give me a headache. "I haven't thought much about what Washington had to face besides battles. I can see it was more complex than what I usually read in my history book. I have heard a lot about Boston and the Tea Party. Philadelphia is also prominent in the history books for the Liberty Bell and the Declaration of Independence. Was New York really that important?"

"Actually, New York was what you might call pivotal. It was a major port city in the middle of the colonies with a lively shipping trade. When the British captured it, the colonies were effectively split in half. It also had a very strong Tory population to support the British occupation."

"What's a Tory, Gramps? You've used that word before."

"Tories were those who supported the British rule while the Americans who supported independence were called Whigs or Patriots. Doesn't your history book say anything about this?"

"Let's just say I don't remember much about it," I had to admit. "I just thought most Americans wanted independence."

"There were no real surveys to determine exactly how many colonists wanted to separate from the mother country. Those in Massachusetts showed how much they disliked the taxes by the Tea Party and the Battles of Lexington and Concord. In New York there were many who wanted to be independent but also a large group, perhaps even a majority, who wanted to stay with Britain. That's why the British chose to use New York as a beachhead to divide the territory and invade Pennsylvania and the southern colonies. The irony is that when the British occupied the area, they seemed to treat most colonists badly. That resulted in driving many loyal Tories over to the other side."

"That doesn't exactly sound Phi Beta Kappa. So it seems that America was making up its mind as to what it wanted to be, and the British were shooting themselves in the foot."

"That actually describes it very well, Greta. The idea of people ruling instead of a king or dictator was not very common. Britain itself had a form of government by the people. You've heard of the Magna Carta where King John was forced to give up some of his power. In a way, Britain was one of the pioneers of rule by the people. Outside of that I can't think of many examples of democracy."

"So, you are saying America was like a prototype of democracy?"

"It wasn't the first by any means. I believe that in ancient Athens all the men voted in what was a democracy. Still, you could show that the United States has been very unique in the world for the democracy that we have. We are far from perfect, but even people who criticize America would rather live here than in any other country."

"I guess I really haven't thought about all that. I have often heard the saying, 'No taxation without representation.' I just thought everybody wanted England to leave us alone. I knew we had some great leaders, especially Washington."

"Yes, Washington was an amazing fellow. Did you know that after the war there was some talk about making him king? He wasn't interested. Even King George, when he was told about Washington's refusal to be made king said, 'Then he is truly the greatest of men.' I don't want to change the subject or go back to more unpleasant topics, but it seems like there is a dark SUV that has been right behind us for a number of miles."

I turned in my seatbelt to get a look at the car following us. "I can't really see much from here. One dark car just looks like another to me," I said.

"I have been going with the flow of traffic while in the middle lane, so I think I will slide over to the right and go a little slower and see what our mysterious friend does." Gramps moved into the right lane and eased up on the gas peddle. The SUV in the middle lane slowed to keep pace with us. The windows of the mysterious car had a dark tint to them so I couldn't see what the driver looked like or whether there were any passengers. The SUV matched our Jeep's speed for about a mile and then it accelerated and passed us as if late for an appointment.

"Now that was really suspicious," said Gramps. "I keep thinking we must be imagining things, but that car seemed to be matching our speed whether medium or slow. Then, when it became obvious that we were looking at it, they sped off like they were an emergency vehicle."

"That just gives me the creeps," I said. "What do you make of it, Gramps?"

"Well, I don't think we are in any real danger. We also hid the trunk pretty well in the basement before we left. I think at our next stop I'll call Sergeant Muldoon back home and ask him to drive by the house just to check on things while we are gone. In the meantime, let's not let anything spoil our trip. What do you say, kiddo?"

"I'm with you Gramps — literally. Research can be fun, but I sure would like to stop at the fair on the way back. What have we got to lose?"

"You know you have always been able to talk me into most anything — within reason. I have to have an out though. If we have the time on the way back we will definitely do it."

"Cool beans, Gramps. Now we can talk about this mystery — the Box of Secrets. I have always been interested in history, but when you hear some new things and see some places it seems to take on a fresh look."

"That's right, Greta. We don't always learn from the mistakes of the past, but we could."

"How much further is it to Queens?"

Gramps gave me a sideways smile. "Just you relax, and we will get there before you know it."

12
The Lady Spy

There were many heroes during the Revolutionary War. Each soldier had a part to play. Greta and I were finding out about the spies and other military actions in the New York area. The bravery of officers and enlisted were very much on display. There was also the logistics of managing and supplying a war. General Washington had taken up headquarters at Stephen Moore's Red House, which was a part of West Point. Washington was forced to use civilian homes and he made every effort to reimburse the owners for their property.

*   *   *

The horse trotted at a brisk clip up to the Red House where Benjamin Tallmadge dismounted and held the reins out to a stable hand. He was anxious to see his commanding officer to give the latest dispatch. Colonel Hamilton opened the door and ushered Major Tallmadge inside. "Go right in, Benjamin. His Excellency wants to see you." Tallmadge stepped through the hallway and was greeted by Washington.

"Tallmadge, my good man, would you like some tea?"

"No thank you, sir. I am quite content. Here is the latest dispatch from Culper." Washington took the papers from Tallmadge and walked over to his desk. He slit open the envelope and spread the papers out on a nearby table. He opened a trunk and obtained a vial of fluid and began the process of revealing the communication. All was quiet as Washington continued to apply reagent to one of the pages. Then after a minute longer he held up the page to be able to focus on it in the candlelight. Looking over the page at Tallmadge, he spoke.

"Relax Major, this could take a while." Tallmadge removed his hat and tucked it under his arm. "If I may say so, General, you seem to be in rather good spirits today."

"Actually, Benjamin, the whole camp is in excellent spirits after General Wayne's victory at Stony Point. His leadership during that action was inspiring for our officers and men alike. It has given morale new life. Wayne performed admirably and brought us a much needed win." A faint smile played over Tallmadge's face. "I see you are amused, Major. Can you share the reason with me?"

"Forgive me, General. Are you aware of the name some of the men are applying to General Wayne?"

"I am well aware, Major, that he is being referred to as 'Mad Anthony Wayne.' Yes, that may be amusing, but I don't see it as being derogatory. He showed valor during the battle that I believe his men have recognized. In fact, he suffered a head wound, but he determined not to perish by it. Instead he called out to his troops and rallied them to victory. Would that we had more soldiers as mad as Anthony Wayne."

The general continued to brush on the liquid reagent. Then, once again, he looked up.

"Is there something else on your mind, Major?"

"Yes, sir. Culper mentioned to me that his expenses in this business are adding up. He is in need of some coin."

Washington stood and crossed to the other side of the room where a wooden chest sat on the floor. He pulled a key from his pocket and unlocked the chest. As he lifted a bag from inside the chest, Tallmadge could hear the unmistakable clink of coins. Washington opened the bag and removed silver coins consisting of British Sterling. Replacing the bag he turned to Tallmadge. "We don't want to be remiss in paying our debts. We will be able to give a larger sum before long, Major. In the meantime if there were some way to hasten Culper's dispatches it would add to the value. Information is important, but timely information is worth a king's ransom."

*   *   *

The historical record leaves many gaps about what took place in New York during the Revolution. Greta and I were going to find out a great deal regarding the members of the Culper spy ring. We knew some of the names of the players and some of the events. We also knew that loyalties were divided even between families. There were conversations that we let our imagination color in for us. Take for example when two sisters sat together one day drinking coffee.

*   *   *

Two young ladies sat at the table by the window in the coffeehouse. One of the ladies was very animated in the discussion.

"Sarah, sometimes you amaze me with your strange ideas. I hesitate to add that your ideas truly border on rebelliousness.

Where do your sympathies lie?" The eyes of the younger sister glistened with her passionate speech and revealed why many British officers gravitated to her company.

"Now Margaret, I am still a loyal subject to the king, but sometimes I think he is too far away to understand his colonists. I do admit that I was moved to tears when I saw that young man hang three years ago."

"You should never have gone to see that wicked man die. He deserved his punishment," Margaret lectured.

"Yes, I suppose he deserved it, but he was not a wicked man. You should have heard him when he spoke. I can't help thinking he was a man of great courage. He was also too young to meet his death. He was barely more than a beardless boy."

"What would Father say if he heard you speaking like this? He would be sorely vexed, I am sure."

"Yes, he would be vexed, and I could never disappoint Father in what I do. He needs me now more than ever. I just wish there was something I could do to end these atrocities."

"There can be only one end to this nightmare. The colonists have to come to their senses and swear allegiance to the king. Then we can get back to normal and start to have parties and balls like we did before."

"Oh Sister, I believe you concern yourself far too much with frivolous things while the world we live in is chaotic and ruinous. There are still balls, and you go to all of them."

"And you, dear Sister, dwell on morbid topics and refrain from the delights to be found in truly living. How will you ever find an appropriate match to be your husband if you don't attend the gala balls? Where will you meet someone?"

"Excuse me, ladies. Here is your coffee and pitcher of cream. We are short on sugar this morning."

"Thank you, Robert. Oh, before you go, can you answer a question for us?"

"I will certainly try, Miss Margaret. What would you like to know?"

"What was your opinion of the late Mr. Hale?"

"Well, miss, as you know, he was caught as a spy and suffered the fate that was due him. I don't have any great insight into this young man. His youth may be his excuse for choosing the side he did. Now if you will excuse me?"

"Thank you, Robert."

After their server left, Margaret turned to her sister and said, "He is not very handsome, is he?"

"Oh Margaret, you think far too much about outward appearance. I have heard that gentleman converse with others, and I think he is very intelligent and thoughtful. I don't think he really trusted our discretion to share his true feelings on Mr. Hale."

"You could be right, my dear. It is not safe to speak openly here if you do not have strong loyalties to the Crown. I am concerned that things you say may be heard by others. At the very least it would never do for Father to hear of your sympathies toward the rebels."

"I understand, Margaret, but remember that they are only sympathies. I am still a loyal subject. At least I am loyal to Father."

"Sarah, I must go and meet with Major Andre. Are you ready to go?" Margaret took a long sip of her coffee.

"Oh Sister, I do believe you see too much of the Major. I suspect that he may be using you for some nefarious purpose."

"Nonsense, my dear. We are simply friends, and he has introduced me to many interesting people. He was also an excellent dance partner at the last ball given by General Howe. It wouldn't do to ignore such gentlemen as he. Now let us be going before the hour passes."

"No, you go ahead without me. I am to meet Father nearby in an hour, so I will just stay here for the time being. We will see each other at dinner. Take care, my dear."

A few minutes later Robert came to the table again. "Would you like more coffee, miss?" Then he began to speak in a low voice. "I apologize for hearing some of your conversation, miss. I want you to understand that I share your feelings. Mr. Hale was a most unfortunate man, and I do admire his courage. I just can't openly speak of it, as you will understand."

She looked at him more closely and said, "I understand. Thank you for confiding in me. It's not easy or safe these days to be open about how one believes. Do you think these harsh times will ever end?"

"Yes, I do, and I am hoping they will end sooner rather than later."

"I understand you are a pacifist, sir. Would you ever be willing to take up arms for a cause you believe strongly in."

"Miss, you are right to understand that I am a pacifist and would never fire a pistol at another human being or run someone through with a saber. Nevertheless, please don't think me so shallow as to not have strong beliefs and a desire for what is right and just to prevail in the world."

"But if you have strong beliefs, do you simply wait and hope your beliefs will win out in the end? Will not your beliefs and pacifism be overcome by the pistol and saber?"

"Your argument is strong, miss, but give me the compliment of knowing that I have considered this heretofore. Also, miss, I will confide in you that there are ways to support one's beliefs that do not include personally firing a shot or shedding blood. I trust to your discretion not to draw me out further."

"In that case, sir, I will retire for the time being. Let me give you this assurance, though. The thoughts you share with me will never pass to others who might misunderstand and cause you concern. I bid you adieu."

"Yes, miss, adieu. It has been a pleasure."

The young lady stood and softly exited the coffeehouse leaving Robert with his thoughts. He had never spoken so openly to anyone even intimating that he might have a part in the strife that had taken possession of the land. He now had a fear that this beautiful young lady might understand and betray his feelings. But no, it was not fear. It was actually excitement. He had observed this young lady on several occasions and felt that she possessed the strongest character he could imagine. He also believed what she said. She would never cause him harm by repeating something he had said. Yes, he could trust her discretion and rest easy.

As Sarah stepped out onto the street, she began to review the interesting conversation she had just had. She was not inclined to discuss ideas with men she was not acquainted with. This Robert Townsend was someone she found interesting, though. He was a Quaker and most of the time seemed very reserved. He was intelligent and more than just a servant in the coffeehouse. She knew he owned a part of the business with James Rivington. He also held a bookkeeper's position in a nearby business, so he must have a head for finances. She couldn't help feeling there was much more underneath the surface of the man. He seemed to pay attention to the conversations around the coffeehouse but rarely participated in them. She didn't think it was because he was shy. There was something else going on. Was he hiding something? Was he running from his past? Did he come to the city to forget some past sin or was it something else? She couldn't decide.

"Oh Father, there you are. I have been looking all over for you." Sarah took her father's arm, and the two proceeded down the walkway.

"And how is my fair lady this evening?" he asked with a smile.

"To be candid, Father, I am in a rather uneasy mood. It is my sister, sir. Sometimes I believe Margaret lacks an understanding of the troubles of the day. She can go to parties and balls and have a jolly time even though the officers she dances with may perish the next day."

"Tut-tut, my dear. Would you have her spend her youth in somber solitude because a pack of rebels is on the loose? She should enjoy life while she may."

"I understand what you are saying, Father, but I can't help but feel the weight of the times." The two walked arm in arm in silence for half a minute. "Father, don't think me impertinent, but do you really believe the rebels have no reasons for their actions?"

He stopped abruptly and turned toward Sarah showing her a very stern countenance. "My dear, I am surprised at you. You know as well as I do that God has given kings the divine right to rule over us. God rules over us in heaven while kings rule over us on earth. No man should tell a king what to do or not to do. No man should tell a king not to tax him."

"But Father, the Patriots are asking to have some representation like other British subjects. Should not all British subjects be represented in Parliament? Wouldn't that be fair and just?"

"Ah Sarah, that is where the problem lies. Don't call them Patriots. The rebels did not ask. They simply disobeyed the king's laws. Now those laws have to be brought to bear on them. Yes, it is sad, my dear. These are troubling times, but this rebellion will soon be put down. Then you may enjoy life as freely as your sister."

"Are you so certain this will end soon, Father? So many have perished already, and I don't see General Washington giving up so easily. He seems to be like a fox who keeps eluding the hounds."

"Yes, my dear, he is very much like a fox. He is wily and hides very well. But you have never been on a fox hunt. I have, and all fox hunts end the same way." He paused to allow his next statement more force. "The fox always loses. Now let us speak of this no more."

13
A Queens Visit

Some teenagers don't converse very easily with older folks. My parents always encouraged our family to spend time with the elderly. We would go to assisted living facilities just to talk to the residents. I have friends who would never visit one of those places in their wildest imagination. They think the residents can't really talk on their level. I think my friends are missing out. Sometimes it's important to be able to talk on someone else's level. It can surprise you what you can learn. Our visit with the Kims was fabuloso.

"It's so good to see you, Joshua. And who is this lovely young girl with you?" Steven Kim opened the door and ushered us inside.

"This is my granddaughter, Greta. She is keeping track of me while Julie is away helping our daughter with a newborn. Greta's parents are away on a trip as well, so it works out."

"I am pleased to meet you, Mr. Kim," I said politely.

"Keeping track of you must be quite a chore, Joshua," Mr. Kim said while winking at me. "Well, I won't belabor that point. Let's just enjoy the time together. Eileen is making some of her fabulous seafood soup so you won't starve while you are with us. Let's step into the living room."

As we made our way inside, we couldn't help but notice the Korean decor. The rug was burnt orange with flowers woven into it. The mantel held two figurines. One was an elderly woman carrying a basket and the other was an old man with a round straw hat holding a stick.

"I have been looking forward to the flavors of your home, Steven. I must admit, though, I have come on another errand also."

"That doesn't surprise me, Joshua. You always seemed to have many ideas going on in that mind of yours. You mentioned on the phone that you are doing some research. How can I help?"

"We are looking for information about James Rivington's *Royal Gazette*. We recently came across some pages that may have been a part of it, and we just wanted to do a little background checking. You are a professor of history and live in Queens, so I thought you might have some inside information."

"*Retired* professor of history to be accurate. I assume you have done some Internet searches already, but you have come to the right place. James Rivington was a fascinating individual. If you have found some clippings from his *Gazette*, I would consider that a spectacular find. For several years he published the news in the young colonies. He tried to publish the news without bias, but his presses were destroyed by some Patriots who didn't like his defending King George. Then he moved to New York and published the *Gazette*, which was the revolutionary version of what we hear today called 'fake news.' It was definitely in favor of the Crown, but the story doesn't stop there. Forgive my monologue, young lady, but 'old' professors have to take advantage of the audiences they get."

"Oh, do go on, Professor Kim," I encouraged him. "I appreciate hearing about this."

"After the war when most Tories left for England or Canada Rivington stayed in New York. Many say he was even visited by General Washington himself. This gave rise to speculation that he was actually working for Washington all along. Yes, indeed, James Rivington was quite a character."

"When you say 'working for General Washington,' do you mean as a spy himself?"

"That is exactly what I mean, Joshua. You must have heard by now of the Culper spy ring."

"Yes," Gramps replied, "and we have been doing some reading about it, but go ahead and tell us what you know."

"It is a fascinating tale of espionage, Joshua. I published a paper about the Culper ring back when I was toiling in the mines of historical academia. Washington had learned the value of inside information when he fought in the French and Indian War. Then when he was forced to flee New York by the British Army and their naval power, he knew that he couldn't just give up on the area if the Revolution was to ever be successful. He picked men to head up what today we call intelligence operations. He first picked Nathaniel Sackett and then Charles Scott. Later on he selected Benjamin Tallmadge, who turned out to be the perfect choice. Tallmadge knew the area, having been raised in Setauket on Long Island. He also had a plan. He started with a man named Abraham Woodhull, who had been a neighbor of his in Setauket. Woodhull was a farmer and was already traveling into the city to sell his goods. It was a great cover story. Woodhull went by the code name of Samuel Culper, which is why the ring was called the Culper spy ring."

"But why call it a ring, Steven?"

"Because there were a handful of others involved with Woodhull. Caleb Brewster would often carry the correspondence via his whaleboat across the Sound. Sometimes Brewster would even ride to Washington's camp if the information was urgent. Austin Roe was also a courier. It wasn't until the 1900s that the name of another member of the ring became known. Robert Townsend was what you might call the inside agent. He lived in the city and could collect information and then pass it on to Woodhull or Brewster or Roe for delivery to Washington. Usually it went to Tallmadge, who would be the one to personally give it to Washington. That was part of the beauty of the ring. Not even Washington knew who was in the ring. That became the only cloak of protection when Benedict Arnold defected to the British side. If Washington had known the name of the ring members, then Arnold would have known their names. They would have been arrested and hung for treason when Arnold defected. So you see Joshua, in many ways espionage began to come of age with the Culper spy ring during the Revolutionary War."

"How so, Steven? Spying was common in recorded history. Moses sent twelve spies into Canaan to see if they could conquer the land. Rahab later hid spies to protect them."

"Oh Joshua! Don't think that espionage didn't change between the time of Moses and James Bond."

"Of course it changed," I said joining into the conversation. "James bond had fast cars and an arsenal of weapons."

"I am not talking about technology, young lady. I am talking about methods and strategy."

"Okay, Steven. What did the Culper ring do that Moses did not."

"To begin with, only Tallmadge knew the names of the ring members. Secondly, only Woodhull and possibly Roe and Brewster knew Townsend's name. Washington knew him only as Culper junior."

"Nice! Mr. Kim, I was doing some research about this and they used numbers as a code to encrypt their messages."

"That's right, young lady. They had a code for some of the people and places. They also went one step further." He paused to let the next thought sink in. "They used invisible ink."

"Slick! But how did they read it?" I asked.

"They had to use a chemical referred to as a reagent to make the ink visible. They would write messages between the lines of other letters or inside book covers. Then, when Washington got the paper, he would apply the reagent and voila."

"That sounds like a lot of trouble. Why not just use the code so no one could figure it out?"

"Well, Greta, if a messenger was stopped on the road and a letter he was carrying had code numbers in it, then he could be made to talk and then hung as a spy."

"Yes, of course. The invisible ink was a necessity."

"So can you tell me why you are so interested in espionage and the Culper spy ring, Joshua?"

"We found the Rivington page in an old trunk that may have belonged to someone during the Revolution. There are also some men of questionable character who are interested in the trunk, and they think it might be valuable."

"Are there any distinguishing marks on the trunk?"

"We have checked the style, and it looks like it may be from the 1800s. There are also the initials *RT* on a metal plate on the trunk."

"Oh I see. Well, if that trunk is connected with the Culper ring, it is interesting to note that the initials *RT* could belong to Robert Townsend. What else did you find in the trunk?"

"Just an old book," I exclaimed.

"Not just any old book," added Gramps. "It looks like an early edition of Thomas Paine's pamphlet, *Common Sense.*"

Professor Kim let out a long, low whistle. "You may indeed be tying puzzle pieces together with that one. You see, *Common Sense* has been suggested as one of the key reasons that Robert Townsend became a spy. It was a great influence on him. Townsend was a Quaker, and as such was against violence and war. That book was written by a Quaker and justified taking up arms against the Crown."

"Well, Professor, I knew we had come to the right place for answers."

"But why come to me, Joshua? You could have found out most of this by Googling it."

"True enough, Steven, but I wanted Greta to hear your personal history, and I think it has bearing on our understanding of the

Revolution. She knows now that many Colonists had assimilated into a new identity as Americans while many still held to the old loyalties. You came to America as a young Korean, but I believe you feel like an American."

"Yes, that's right, Joshua. I was born in what is now a part of North Korea in 1931. Korea had been controlled by Japan since 1910, and they taught us to hate the West. In grade school we set up dolls of Roosevelt, Churchill, Chiang Kai Shek, and MacArthur to attack them in effigy with our pine bayonets. We were always victorious." Steven broadened into a smile at his joke.

"I can picture that happening Steven. Japan controlled much of the Far East."

"Then, in 1945, Japan surrendered and Korea began to have internal conflicts. The North was communist-controlled while the South had more freedom with democracy. North and South Korea set up separate governments and both claimed to rule the whole of Korea. At the age of fifteen, I knew I could not fight for the communist North."

"Why was that, Mr. Kim? How was the North so different?"

"In the North an education was out of the question. The government believed an educated citizen was a danger to it. I escaped to the South and found myself in the army there. Then someone informed my superiors that I was from the North and must be a spy. I was arrested and interrogated to the point of torture for fifty-one days. At last they released me. Once again I fought for freedom's cause. Finally, the war ended in 1953. Then in 1965 I came to Portland, Oregon."

"So why did you come to America, Mr. Kim?"

"Perhaps it was for the same reason many British came to America. Everyone knew it was the land of opportunity. You should also realize that it was not easy to come here. The Korean war ended in 1953, but I did not make it to America until 1965. It took twelve years to come over. I brought my wife over three years later."

"Did you become citizens, Mr. Kim?"

"Yes, of course, my dear. It was a great privilege."

"Did you feel like you were losing something by no longer being Korean?" I asked.

"Oh, not at all. I am still Korean and always will be. I did not swear hatred to Korea. I swore allegiance to America. I still love my culture of Korea. I also believe in the American Constitution and form of government. America was the land of opportunity in the 1700s and the 1900s and it is the same today. That opportunity is not in the soil. It is in the ideals of freedom and justice for all. I must humbly add that God has been very gracious to Eileen and me." The professor stopped himself at this point. "You really have me going now. I might just run for Congress."

"We would vote for you," I affirmed.

The professor paused for a moment and then switched topics. "One more item might interest you two."

"We are all ears, Professor."

"There was a member of the Culper spy ring who has never been identified."

"And who do you think he was, Steven?"

"Actually, he was a she. She was always referred to as Agent 355. Remember code numbers were used, and 355 was used for her. There has been a lot of speculation about her, but no one knows who she was. We believe she was a lady who could move in high society and collect some useful information."

"When you say 'lady,' I don't think you simply mean female."

"No, I mean she was either from a wealthy or a powerful family or both. You see, the codebook used by the spy ring had another number for female but used 355 for a lady. Besides that, is the fact that the type of information gained would have been obtained from officers or gentlemen. It would not have come from lower-ranking soldiers of the king."

"And you say her identity has never been found out?" I asked.

"There have been a number of suggestions, but none that seem to be a true fit for this brave lady. We may never know her name. Ah, it looks like Mrs. Kim is coming with the soup. Are we ready to eat?"

"I am famished, Mr. Kim," I had to admit. With that we moved in the direction of the aroma.

14

Culper Jr. and Agent 355

Greta and I were intrigued by what Professor Kim had said about the Culper spy ring. In particular, we wondered about Agent 355 and who she could have been. While I visited with the Kims, Greta went online looking for more clues to the identity of that brave lady. One suggestion was Anna Strong, but, while she was a member of the spy ring, she was a known Patriot and could not have been privy to military intelligence. Agent 355 must have had connections with the Crown that made her beyond suspicion.

We may never know the identity of this female agent, but I had a feeling Greta was going to make her computer give up the answer if she could. It wasn't long before Greta had a psychological and social profile of the lady.

The stereotype of a female spy is a raving beauty who can knock the stuffing out of men and then blow them a kiss while she rides off into the sunset. A modern spy named Christine Granville was described in *The Guardian* as a charming beauty who was fast-thinking, brave, devoted, and instinctive.

Beauty may indeed be up to the beholder, but you would think that charm would be a necessity for Agent 355. She had to have interaction with British officers or Tory politicians. A character flaw of some men is to inflate their own importance by sharing their knowledge with an interested female.

This lady had to be courageous to face the gallows if caught. The year 1777 was known by all as the year of the hangman. The hangman's noose was not a respecter of persons male or female. She would have been intelligent and resourceful. She was so discreet in her activities that her identity has not been discovered to this day.

*   *   *

The young man stepped out of the door and turned the key to lock up the shop of Templeton and Stewart. He was a bookkeeper as well as being part owner of the nearby coffeehouse. He turned to see a lady with several packages in her hand walking just past the shop.

"Miss Sarah, may I help you with those packages?"

"Ah, thank you, Mr. Townsend, is it you? I will allow you to carry my packages while I hold the umbrella. It does seem to rain on a moment's notice. I was supposed to meet my sister here, but she seems to be late today."

"I have to admit to thinking that her loss is my gain."

"Mr. Townsend, I did not imagine you to be so forward."

"Forgive me, miss. I would not put you off for the world. I mean no disrespect," Robert quickly assured her. "I simply appreciate your conversation. It is more thoughtful than most I meet here in the city."

"I take that as a compliment, Mr. Townsend, and I will reply that you are more sober-minded than most I meet here. I consider that a virtue that I find less frequent in these troubling times."

The two walked along for perhaps a hundred yards without further discourse. Then the lady spoke in a soft voice.

"These are indeed troubling times, Mr. Townsend, and I wish I could be a cause of resolving the conflict as you are doing."

"I don't know what you mean, miss," Robert sounded startled.

"I think you do, Mr. Townsend. I have seen how you observe the events in the coffeehouse as well as in the town. You seem to have many things on your mind besides just business. I have also noticed you passing envelopes on to Mr. Roe on occasion. Can you deny it, sir?"

At that moment an officer wearing a red coat approached them from the opposite direction. He touched his hat toward the lady with unexpected politeness and both nodded toward him. He went on his way while the couple continued to walk together. The two walked along for another fifty feet before the lady spoke again.

"Please do not be alarmed, Mr. Townsend. I would not betray you to even my own family when I am confident they would do you harm. No, I could do you no injury, Mr. Townsend." Once again the two were silent as they walked. Then Robert began to speak in low tones and very deliberately.

"Miss Sarah, I believe you to be completely honest and virtuous. Even so, I cannot be entirely open with you about your suspicions. If you are correct, then my well-being may be hanging by a mere thread that could eventually be replaced by a cord of hemp. No, Miss Sarah it is because I admire you that I must not give you that responsibility."

She did not hesitate in her response. "It is because I admire you, Mr. Townsend, that I make this speech. Your reply has been guarded but you have not denied my assertions. In so doing I am more confident than ever that my assertions are true. I do not wonder that you are reluctant to confess your private mission to me. I cannot forget the fate of the young officer Hale. His memory has haunted me for these three years. His courage has also inspired me and has done more so." She hesitated only a moment before adding, "I have changed my opinion of the cause I believe you share with him. I have seen how the king's men have treated one and all in a most villainous way. My ears have heard of the infamous Colonel Simcoe and his atrocities. I have come to the point of wanting to aid the cause you serve. I also believe I can trust you even though you are reluctant to trust my sincerity." Another pause followed before Sarah spoke again. "There are times when I hear things in the city or in your coffeehouse or from my sister or father that I believe would be valuable to the Patriot cause. I will be giving you that information to do with it what you will."

Once again the two walked on in silence. The hour was now late. The street was getting dark with few pedestrians about. Then Robert slowly turned to his companion.

"Miss Sarah, your trust in me is a great honor that I am unworthy of. Do not doubt that I admire your courage and openness to me. Your honesty has never been a question in my mind. It is because of that honesty that my words are guarded. Were you to be questioned by your father or a British officer, you could not refrain from speaking and answering the truth. It is for that reason that my words have been guarded toward you. I cannot, nay I must not, be more open with you."

"Mr. Townsend, though you may guard yourself around me, I do have occupations that make me aware of information that could be beneficial to the cause I believe we both now share. I will also confide in you that if I become aware of missions that are undertaken by the ones who wear red, then I may be able to transfer that knowledge to your ears. You, in turn may give voice to those whom you see fit to inform."

"Miss Sarah, I am overcome with emotion at what you have been suggesting. If I were involved in a business so truly dangerous in these times I could not under any circumstances allow you to take risks that would bring danger if you were also to be involved. I cannot allow you to do so."

A smile now radiated from Sarah's face, and she quietly replied, "I believe you have misunderstood something, Mr. Townsend. I am not asking your permission to be involved. I am letting you know that if Providence gives me information pertinent to this cause, I will give you that information to do with as you think fit. I am not giving you the choice in the matter."

He was very much taken aback by her boldness. There were times he had been afraid of the dangers he faced. He had bolstered his own courage by thinking himself strong enough to face the task. He had wondered how many men would be brave enough to carry out these missions like he was doing. Now he was with a young lady who showed no fear. She even exceeded the virtues he had always suspected of her.

The two looked into each others eyes with a newfound realization. They now had a link between them. They were not merely acquaintances or simply friends. This was not a social arrangement. They were now involved in a mission together. They now shared a belief and a cause, and they both knew the dangers. If one was unfaithful to what had been said, the other could suffer consequences. Without speaking further, they continued to walk, lost in their thoughts about what had transpired.

Robert reviewed his opinion of her. She was lovely in form, and he knew her to be virtuous and of high moral character. He now realized that her thoughts went far deeper into the events of the times. She had the intellect to see through his ruse. She suspected what he actually was — a spy. She also had the courage to suggest that she could help him in this dangerous work. He was shocked at her willingness.

For her part, Sarah felt his words confirmed her opinion of him. Robert possessed a quiet strength. He put himself at risk for a cause that would touch millions of lives on both sides of the Atlantic. He had not asked for her help. In fact, he had declined her offer since she would also be at risk. Her life had now been forever changed. She felt her life was an extension of Nathan Hale's and Robert Townsend's and many others. She had spoken of Providence, and now she believed that God was behind this movement. This pacifist Quaker had put his life on the line for the cause of freedom, and she wished to do the same. Indeed, she could do no less.

"Hello, my dear, is that you?" Sarah's father called out, jolting the two companions from their thoughts.

"Oh yes, Father. Here am I. Are you acquainted with Mr. Townsend?"

"Yes, of course. Good evening, Robert. I see you are helping Sarah with her packages. How good of you."

"It has been my good fortune to be of this small service, sir."

"I thank you for your kindness, Robert. I believe I can accompany her from here if you have other matters to attend to."

"Certainly, sir. It has been a pleasure, Miss Sarah." He tipped his cap to father and daughter and turned back in the direction of his shop. As he walked, along he felt the adrenaline rush of his recent conversation. He had never spoken so openly with someone regarding his dangerous work. For that matter, he had never had so intimate a conversation with a lady before. He realized that she knew enough about him to report to the British authorities if she so desired. But he had confidence in her that she would not. All the stories he had heard about the fickle female heart for some reason did not apply to Sarah. In his estimation, she was one of a kind.

15
Oyster Bay and Setauket

O ur visit with the Kims had been perfect in every way. Gramps was able to renew their friendship, and I got to drink in the history. I appreciated Professor Kim's personal background the most. We hear a lot about North Korea today. It was enthralling to talk to someone who had come from there. The Kims had lived through some trying times and had come to a land of promise to live out a dream.

I thought about how fortunate I really was. My life had always been safe and secure. My parents were tops, and my family was always supportive of activities I wanted to do. They were supportive as long as I didn't want to do anything illegal, immoral, or too expensive. Then there was Gramps and Gram. I knew that my friends loved their grandparents as well. I just couldn't believe anybody could have grandparents as great as mine. Oh well, I guess I must be really biased.

Gramps and I had driven from Queens to Oyster Bay. Our plan was to go to Setauket later that day. We wanted to see firsthand where Robert Townsend and Abraham Woodhull had called home. "Oh Gramps," I said, "history just seems to be more real when you travel there and look at the places of the people you have been studying about."

"That's right, kiddo. Of course, a lot has changed since Woodhull and Townsend set foot in this area. It was mostly farmland back then with a few houses dotting the landscape. The towns were small villages with just the essential commerce going on. Travel was a lot slower then, too. Going fifty miles into New York City was the better part of a day. That's why Woodhull had to stay over at his brother-in-law Amos Underhill's house when he rode into town."

"I like horses, Gramps, but it is nice to be able to drive five or six hundred miles in a day instead of just fifty. It must have taken a long time for a spy report to get back to Washington."

"Yes, communication has gone through many changes since that time with the advent of technology. Back then it usually took a week for information to get all the way from Culper junior in the city to General Washington at his headquarters. It was a source of irritation for the General. He kept asking for Tallmadge to make the route shorter and faster, but speed would have put the ring under suspicion. One week was actually pretty fast. Originally, it took two weeks to get reports all the way to Washington. Then there were periods of time that the ring was silent because of increased scrutiny by the British."

"What do you mean by increased scrutiny, Gramps?"

"In one of Tallmadge's communications with General Arnold he intimated that there was a contact in the city who gave them information. Then when Arnold defected, he pushed for more interrogations of people there trying to find out who that was. There were more checkpoints along the road to look for suspicious travelers."

"What's our first stop, Gramps?"

"If we went chronologically according to the Culper spy ring, we would start with Woodhull in Setauket. Since we are driving from Queens, however, we will go geographically to Oyster Bay first and see Robert Townsend's home, which is called Raynham Hall. Townsend went by the code name of Culper junior. Woodhull, who was Culper senior, recruited Townsend because he felt it was too dangerous for him to keep going back and forth into New York City. Townsend was working in the city at a local shop before he bought into Rivington's coffee shop so he could work there and pick up information from the patrons. When people go out to relax at a restaurant or coffeehouse, they like to talk. Townsend liked to listen."

"Speaking of food, I'm hungry, Gramps. Can we get a burger before we get there?"

"We can certainly scratch that itch. The normal hours for the Raynham Hall Museum is 1:00 to 5:00 in the afternoon. I believe they will have a docent there who will be knowledgeable about the Hall and Townsend's involvement. We can kill an hour getting something to eat and then get to the Hall."

"You got me on that one, Gramps. What's a docent?"

"It's a fancy name for a guide. It's someone who will be knowledgeable but often is there as a volunteer."

After burgers, fries, and cold drinks, we followed the GPS to Raynham Hall and parked on the west side. A minute later we knocked on the door of the museum. For the next hour, the docent led us around and we got to know the history of the house as well as the family. The docent told us that "Solomon Townsend was a sea captain and the older brother of Robert. He had been the most well known of the family until it was discovered that Robert was in actuality the spy known as Culper junior."

I piped up and questioned, "What do you mean 'discovered'? How did they find out?"

"The Culper spies were not looking for notoriety. They did not even apply for a pension after the war to receive an income for the services they rendered. Only Woodhull, Austin Roe, and possibly Tallmadge and Caleb Brewster knew that Robert Townsend was working for Washington. It wasn't until 1930 when historian Morton Pennypacker compared the handwriting of letters sent by Culper junior and Townsend that his identity became known. Until then, Solomon Townsend was the most famous resident of Raynham Hall."

"That looks like a special exhibit, ma'am. What's it all about?"

"Good question, young lady. We call that exhibit The Slave Quarters, and it features the slave Bible that was purchased for the museum."

"You mean slaves had their own Bibles back then," I asked?

"No, that's not what I mean at all. Most slaves could not read and few could purchase a Bible. This one is called the slave Bible because it listed the names of slaves who lived at Raynham Hall. It gives us insight into the family's attitude toward slavery."

"How so, ma'am?" I prodded.

"Well, usually a Bible would only have the names and births and deaths of family members. This Bible listed the names and births of slaves and would have helped them gain their freedom."

"You've got me again, ma'am. How do names in a Bible help give them freedom."

"You are asking the perfect questions, miss. A Bible was as good as a birth certificate to show the age of someone. A slave's age was needed for someone to be set free. It is also noteworthy that all the names were written into this Bible at the same time, according to analysts. They were written in 1795, which was five years after Samuel Townsend had passed away. They may have been written by Robert Townsend, but the evidence is inconclusive."

Gramps then asked, "What more can you tell us about Robert Townsend's personal life, ma'am?"

"I can tell you he never married. He left New York City after the war and lived here with his sister Sally. There was a rumor that he fathered a child with his housekeeper who was named Mary Banvard. That is unlikely, though, and Solomon Townsend years later claimed that their brother William was the actual father. Nevertheless, the boy was named Robert after our Culper hero, and Robert senior took care of him and actually left the boy $500 in his will."

"Excuse me, ma'am," I interrupted. "If Mr. Townsend wasn't known to be in the ring, then he never really got rewarded for being a spy."

"That's right, miss. He didn't apply for a pension, and as far as we know he never got a reward."

*   *   *

After the tour, we were back on the road again. "Raynham Hall is a fascinating place. Don't you think so, Gramps?"

"It certainly is. I kept imagining a group of soldiers led by Colonel Simcoe sharing the house with the family. It was a good-sized home, but having soldiers staying with them must have made it feel very small. The guide was very knowledgeable. She had a great grasp of the spy ring. I was particularly interested in the trunks there."

"Yes, but you have to admit that none of the trunks there looked exactly like ours."

"True, Greta, but the explanation for that is relatively simple."

"And what would that be, Gramps?"

"Trunks or boxes back then were not mass-produced on an assembly line. They were made one at a time by a craftsman. That's why they might be very similar, but you would be hard-pressed to say they were alike. They were all made of wood, and I noticed that one trunk there had a key lock on it."

"Why do you think furniture styles change so much, Gramps?"

"Indeed, styles do change over time. One reason is because manufacturing methods have changed. The cost of raw materials also changes. That's why synthetic materials are used more frequently today than in the past."

"What's our next stop?"

"We are heading to Setauket now, which is the area Abraham Woodhull was from. The north shore of Long Island is a beautiful area, Greta. It is surprising to see a rural community so near a major city like New York City. I have always loved seeing water whether lake, river, or ocean. Strong's Neck was where Anna Strong lived and, according to the tour guide, hung her laundry out to signal Caleb Brewster where he could pick up a dispatch. She must have been a very strong — no pun intended — lady."

"Tell me more, Gramps. What else do we know about Anna Strong?"

"Anna Strong's husband was named Selah. He was imprisoned by the British for part of the war and then left the area with their family. Anna stayed to presumably care for their farm, but as time went by, it seemed she was actively helping Abraham Woodhull. It is said that she acted like Woodhull's wife to travel into town with him. A single man traveling into town aroused suspicion, while a man and wife would be passed through the checkpoints more readily."

"So she did at least two important tasks for the spies," I echoed. "She hung laundry as a signal, and she acted as cover for Woodhull to travel into the city?"

"That's right," said Gramps. "Some have even suggested that Anna Strong was Agent 355."

"That would be really neat," I said. "Don't you think Anna could be a spy?"

"A spy yes, but not Agent 355. You see, there was a definite upswing in the quality of information that the Culper ring was passing after Agent 355 joined the team. That means that Agent 355 must have had some connections with high-ranking British officers or administrators. Anna Strong was the wife of a known prisoner. It is unlikely that anyone would share sensitive information with her."

"So, who do you think Agent 355 was, Gramps?"

"We may never know, Greta. She appears to have been a lady with connections to the British Loyalists. She may have been acquainted with high-ranking officers. She may have been a socialite. Notice the key word here is may. There was also a rumor that Townsend may have had a romantic interest in her. Like I said, we may never know who she was."

"I have to admire her as well as all the American spies. If they had been caught, they would have been hung just like Nathan Hale was. Is it true that the British did espionage for money while the Americans just did it to serve their country?"

"For the most part that is true of the Culpers, Greta. Woodhull kept a ledger of his expenses and asked Washington through Tallmadge to reimburse him. His reimbursements were nothing compared to what the British were paying their secret agents."

"I can't believe that Washington was so stingy with his agents like Woodhull and Townsend. All they wanted was to get reimbursed for what they spent. They were not rich men."

"True enough, Greta, but you have to understand Washington's situation. The British Crown could tax their island people for money to finance military ventures. The Continental Congress really did not have the authority to tax. They could only ask the colonies for assistance and hope for the best. Washington had a real challenge just feeding his men much less paying them."

16

Not So Funny Money

Greta and I were beginning to think of the Culper spy ring as old friends. Professor Kim had given us a thorough rundown of the process. Tallmadge was usually the one who placed the reports directly in George Washington's hand. He picked up the report from a drop made by Caleb Brewster. The young sea dog was usually given a signal from Anna Strong who had been told by Abraham Woodhull where a package could be retrieved. Woodhull received the papers from Austin Roe, who was the courier from New York City itself. The spy ring was fully functional and sent regular reports to the commander-in-chief. He relied on the accuracy of the Culper reports, which were confirmed from other directions. Information was the key word. While all the pieces of the puzzle were essential, none was more important than a quiet man who would wait on tables in Rivington's coffeehouse in New York City.

*   *   *

One November day in 1779 the rich aroma of Colombian coffee filled the air. The coffeehouse patrons sat at three of the six tables. Two of the tables were occupied by local tradesmen while at another table sat two British officers who seemed to be in a rather pleasant mood.

"Ho there, Robert. Be a good chap and take these coffee mugs over to table three." The portly man set two mugs of coffee on the table as he spoke. His friendly manner enabled him to appeal to customers from all walks of life. British officers, society ladies, and local store owners made his shop a popular gathering place.

"Certainly, Mr. Rivington. Did those two officers only order coffee on this day?"

"You know how these gentlemen are. They have spent the night carousing and just need to warm themselves before going out to do more mischief."

Robert winked in acknowledgment and walked off to the two Redcoats with mugs in hand. Setting the coffee down, he said, "Here you are, gentlemen. Do you want a morsel of bread to help face today's tasks?"

The dark-haired officer picked up his mug and said, "What a fine fellow you are, Robert. Only thinking about serving and the simple things in life. Why can't more colonists be like you Quakers? Well, today won't take us far afield. Still, I believe I will have a bit of bread. Do you have a slice of ham to go with it?"

"No sir, of a truth, we have been out of ham for about a week now. We may get some in next week, but I can't be sure, sir. You know how unreliable supplies are."

"Yes, even though it just comes from a few miles away in Long Island. Those Whigs will hold onto the good cuts of pork, beef, and mutton while we go wanting here. Well, just bring me the bread, if you please. Toast it, of course."

"Of course, sir. With toast and imported jam and our fine coffee you will be on your way with a warm, full belly."

When Robert turned and went, the younger officer leaned over to his companion and said, "A fine fellow. What would he say, I wonder, if he knew today's mission could well break the backs of these Whig traitors? I wish I could see Washington's face when he finds out. Wouldn't you like to hear the Continental Congress discuss our new strategy? What about those Adams boys in Boston? I can imagine how red their faces will get when they find out. Can't you see the steam coming out of their ears?"

Robert was passing their order on to the cook, but he was still close enough to pick up the officers' conversation. What could they be up to? he wondered.

Robert had only been in the city for a short time when he got to know James Rivington and joined him in his coffeehouse venture. Rivington was a well-known publisher of a Tory newspaper – *The Royal Gazette*. The *Gazette* printed a version of news that was meant to please the Crown and its loyal subjects living in the New York area. Rivington was a fascinating character. His newspaper was most decidedly pro-British, but there were times that Rivington made comments that made Robert wonder where his loyalties actually lay. Then again, his loyalties might simply go to the highest bidder. Rivington had a very strong mercenary streak in him. He also had a gift to see the humor in life. He published in his newspaper the story of when the Whigs hung him in effigy. He laughed louder than anyone about it with his coffeehouse patrons.

Robert, for his part, was in this coffeehouse with a definite purpose. A Quaker since birth, Robert possessed the pacifist opinion of most Quakers of the time. War or acts of violence were not to be supported. This struggle that held the land in its grasp must be endured but not condoned. He had resided in Oyster Bay on Long Island all his life. His father was considered to be a somewhat liberal Quaker. The senior Townsend dressed in a more stylish manner than the typical Quakers of the day. He had been interested in politics at one time, but the British had taken control of Oyster Bay. The family home was commandeered by the British, who destroyed property and caused many indignations. He was even forced to swear allegiance to the Crown or go to prison. The British prison ships were notorious for mistreatment of prisoners often leading to an untimely death.

Perhaps the greatest influence on Robert Townsend was the son of a Quaker named Thomas Paine. In 1776 he published a pamphlet called *Common Sense,* which entreated the colonists to throw off the yoke of Great Britain. Robert knew he wanted to help end this conflict. As a merchant he would often travel to the city and stay at Amos Underhill's boardinghouse. On occasion he met with Abraham Woodhull, and the two began to share common interests. One night Woodhull had trusted him enough to share a way that could bring an end to this miserable strife. Woodhull said that their wretched taskmasters would be sent packing. Robert did not have to fire a shot or use a bayonet on a hapless foe.

After that night, Robert had taken a share in Rivington's coffeehouse with the intent of collecting information. He knew it was dangerous. If he were found out, his life would be forfeited and his property would be taken by these hated Redcoats. But he believed he had to do something. He had to make a difference.

From across the room, Robert watched the two officers and

wished he could hear what they were saying. Then the dark-haired officer took some paper from his pocket and unfolded it. Both Redcoats began to carefully examine the paper. He wished he could see it. Dare he go back to the table just now? Yes, he must see what this paper was.

"Would you like some fresh coffee, sirs?"

The officer started to put the paper back in his pocket, but then he stopped and held it out. "Ah, Robert, give us your opinion. What do you think of this colonial note here?"

"Of a truth, sir. I am surprised that you would be carrying a colonial note. They aren't worth the paper they are printed on."

Both officers roared with laugher at this remark. Robert did not think his comment so humorous and simply smiled.

"Robert, you have spoken to the point – to the very point. It's the paper that is the key. The paper is very critical when it comes to banknotes. The ink and the plates are important, to be sure, but the paper is critical. A blind man can tell you whether a banknote is genuine by simply touching the paper. It is not by sight but by touch that you can tell if it is genuine. Would you say this is a bona fide note, Robert?"

Robert took the note and rubbed it between his fingers. "I am certainly not experienced in detecting a forgery, sir, but it looks and feels like a real banknote."

"Here, Robert, let us put you to the test." The officer motioned to his companion, who pulled another note from his own pocket. "Here is another Continental dollar. If I were to tell you that one of these is genuine and the other is not, could you tell which is the true note?"

Robert held one note in his left hand and the other in his right. He examined each and rubbed them between his fingers and finally shrugged his shoulders. "By your leave, sirs, I cannot distinguish one from the other."

"Ah, that is the material point, my good man. That is the material point." With that the officer folded both notes and put them in his pocket and lifted his coffee mug.

"To General Washington," he said. "May he enjoy the day – for tomorrow is coming."

As Robert left the table, he was very troubled. He kept pondering the conversation and what it could mean. Later that day he spoke to Rivington about it.

"Ah Robert, you Quakers are indeed a rather naive lot. Those gentlemen are on a mission of great importance. I have a friend who owns a press much like mine, and he has been kept very busy as of late."

"How so, Mr. Rivington?"

"They haven't been printing another newspaper. They are printing money, my good man — colonial dollars."

"But colonial dollars aren't worth much as it is. Why print more of them?"

"Oh Robert, you are such a goose. When there are more dollars by the thousands or even millions, then the currency becomes absolutely worthless. Can you imagine Washington paying his troops with paper? What can a man do with worthless paper besides paper his own house with it? Don't you see! The troops will be paid with worthless paper. Desertion becomes universal. The colonial economy collapses. It could mean the end of the war."

Robert tried to hide his shock at the thought. "But the British have tried to counterfeit before. Why would they succeed now?"

"It's the paper, Robert. They now have the paper."

"What do you mean, sir?"

Rivington gave a long sigh at his friend's simple understanding. "Oh, Robert, the British have obtained the very paper that Congress uses to print colonial dollars with. Using the same paper means that no one can distinguish the original dollars from the ones the British will be flooding the land with." Rivington turned away toward the kitchen leaving Robert with his thoughts.

Robert tried to hide his anxiety. He went about his duties carefully so as to avoid suspicion. As the day drew to a close, Robert took off his apron and put on his coat and hat. He had much to do. Later that evening he put quill to paper and set down the facts as he knew them. He prided himself on getting his facts straight. He needed to get this information into the right hands as quickly as possible. That made him extra cautious. He instinctively realized that for him to act in a peculiar manner would arouse suspicion. He would visit the Underhills in the middle of the night and be back at his shop before dawn. It was risky, but it must be done.

17

Someone Else's Mail

G ramps and I wanted to make one more stop on Long Island. We knew that the black market known as the London Trade went back and forth across the water from New York to Connecticut. We wanted to see what that trip would be like. We were true landlubbers but enjoyed the water whenever we got the chance.

It was a balmy day to be driving on Long Island. We headed to Port Jefferson to catch the ferry. "What's next on our agenda, Gramps? Full disclosure is I am hungry enough to eat your briefcase, so I suggest we keep our eyes peeled for some chow."

"We can have an early dinner and take the ferry across the Sound and back. The Kims are expecting us to spend the night again, and I told them we might be late and thanked them for accommodating us. We don't want to miss the opportunity for a good cup of chowder here, though." We found a seafood place and were not disappointed.

"I have an urge to munch on some clam strips and that seafood chowder smells great," Gramps commented. "It looks like we came to the right place." I ordered a lobster roll since I hadn't eaten one in many months.

"We still have an hour before our ferry departs, Greta. We might as well relax. Let's find a spot where we can sit. Did you notice the candy shop next door?"

My eyes lit up. "You lead, and I will be glad to follow."

We both got sundaes with lots of whipped cream and a cherry on top. I couldn't resist completing our splurge with a bag of goodies. Then Gramps sipped a cup of coffee while I kept looking at the candy behind the counter. Then I remembered something.

"Can I see the letter, Gramps?"

"Which letter do you mean, kiddo?"

"The love letter, of course. It shows us a lot about how the couple felt toward each other."

"Let's get on board the ferry first," said Gramps. "Then you can peruse the letter to your heart's content." A half hour later we had parked the Jeep and purchased tickets for the ferry. I was proud of Gramps for not complaining about the price. Cars were in the car line to take the ferry across the Sound, but we just wanted to make this a round-trip as passengers. The smell of the sea allowed my mind to float and my imagination tried to feel the call of people who went to sea. I had read books like Mutiny on the Bounty but hadn't actually spent a lot of time near the water. I could almost sense that the sea could be very alluring.

Once seated in the passenger compartment I could feel the hum of the engine as we began to move away from the dock. I looked out the window to see a seagull perched on the side of the ship. Further out in the water was a two-masted sailing ship. It all seemed so picture-perfect. Getting up I took a tour of the passenger area. There was a snack bar at one end. Each side of the passenger area was lined with windows to give the full effect of the trip. Long Island was receding at the stern of the ship. To the east was a waterline only broken by a few more ships that were under way. The Connecticut coast was in the distance off the bow. My steps seemed a bit awkward on the moving vessel, so I went back and sat down.

Gramps had brought his satchel from the Jeep and looked through it until he produced the desired letter.

"Be my guest, but just remember you are reading someone else's mail." He winked at me and held out the letter.

I took the paper and began to look it over with great interest. My folks were not shy about being in love. Even Gramps and Gram let me know that age doesn't mean you have to quit being sweet on each other.

"This is really something else, Gramps. Listen to this."

August 22, 1781

To My Dear friend Samuel

These have been trying times for us to live in, Samuel. I know that you have faced dangers beyond what most men could endure. While that danger has given me cause for concern, I also realize it is the very reason our hearts have come together. I think back over the past months and I shudder to think of events which could have had different results. I thank a gracious Providence who has been merciful to each of us.

I must smile when I recall my impressions of you when we met. Of a truth, you had the appearance of a meek and mild-mannered servant. My sister even described you as a quiet one. As the days went by, I came to know that although mild-mannered, you have the heart of a lion. It takes such a heart as well as courage to be able to face the dangers you do and still persevere. You are a perfect blend of strength and humility.

Your history is that of a pacifist, and you would have remained so if not forced to be otherwise. I know you have come to view these troubling times much as I have. Danger seems to be on every side. Men have had their property and liberty and life itself wrested from them. Wives and families have given up their husbands and fathers in a cause that is truly worthy of sacrifice. I think of poor Anna, whose husband was in prison for many months. So many have suffered to greater depths than I could ever imagine. There are times that I yearn to grasp a sword to put up a resistance that these oppressors would understand. That may not be ladylike, but it is how I feel. Then I remember what we are doing and how important our mission really is. That sounds so forward to say "our mission." Do I put you off by claiming that the purpose is a shared one?

Oh, how I pray that God will hasten the day when this wretched war is over. My heart has bled during these times as those we call friends have suffered so much.

Samuel, I do claim you as a dear friend. I would that I could be more help to you. Providence has given the two of us time together and left me with memories that will never fade.

Allow me to leave off from my epistle with a word of caution. Please have a care in your endeavors.

As your admirer, I must now close.

SS

"It is very romantic, Gramps. I don't think I have ever read anything like it before. With email and texting, people don't seem to write letters at all these days. It's a wonder that the US Postal Service even stays open."

 "The post office does stay open, but they have cut back on their hours," Gramps replied. "I agree with you, Greta, that the young lady has felt the pain that war brings to people who are sometimes caught in the middle of it. It is somewhat on the flowery side. No one writes like that nowadays."

"So it seems that Samuel and this SS were doing something together that was for a cause or a mission. Do you think it was something sinister or dangerous?"

"I am not inclined to think it was sinister, but it sounds like it was indeed dangerous."

"And her manner sounds like she was a Patriot. She was sympathetic to his work."

"It may have been even more than that. She believed in the cause for independence, and she was doing things to help that cause."

"Wow, Gramps! Are you saying that she may have been a spy? Do you think that she and Samuel were working together as spies? She wanted to have a real part in the work. She even wanted to pick up a sword and fight. That doesn't sound like ladies from history."

"No, it doesn't, does it. Sometimes we think of women in history as weak and soft. We think they just sat around and had tea parties. Some actually did fight, and there were probably some who wanted to swing a sword like this one." Gramps paused for a moment and then added, "I just had a thought, Greta. Do you remember what our friend Steve said about the unidentified spy?"

"Do you mean the lady spy?"

"Yes. She has simply been referred to as Agent 355 because that is what is recorded by Benjamin Tallmadge to identify this person."

"Are you serious, Gramps? Do you think this letter from SS could be written by the unknown spy?"

"I think it just might be possible. It is written by a lady, and this lady was involved in something dangerous. It may not have been the same spy who was referred to as Agent 355, but then again it just might be."

"It seems like we keep finding out more and more fascinating things about the trunk but not what we really want to know."

"I suppose you mean why Earle and John Henry consider it valuable enough to steal."

"Did you look through the journal yet, Gramps? Did it have anything interesting in it?"

"Yes, I did look through it. Mainly it was a lot of expenses and occasional income notations. You could say it was more a ledger than a journal. It seemed odd to me, but perhaps anyone else's ledger will always seem odd to a stranger reading it."

"What kind of expenses were listed?"

"Well, there were listings for lodging and meals. In a way it made me think this was a ledger for a traveling salesman."

"What about the Bible, Gramps? Did you find out something about that?"

"I believe I did, kiddo. I had never heard of this, but the Bible was printed by Robert Aitken in 1782. It was known as the Bible of the Revolution. Britain had forbidden Bibles to be published in America, insisting that they be imported from the mother country. Actually, it would be more correct to say that Britain wouldn't let Bibles be published in America in English. They were published in other languages. Some were even published in American Indian languages."

"That sounds pretty mean to me. Was it because they could sell them at a higher price and make more money that way?"

"That would be a good guess, kiddo. Then when war broke out and the importation of Bibles was halted, Aitken asked Congress for permission to publish a Bible."

"Wow, Gramps! Are you kidding me? The Bible we found was definitely from the Revolution?"

"Yes, kiddo, indeed it was."

We paused at this point to soak in the sunshine of discovery. Then Gramps brought me back to the present by saying, "We'd better get ready. The ferry will be docking soon."

18
Vive la France

We call the war for independence the American Revolution and rightly so. In our research, Greta and I began to understand the attitude of other nations toward Britain and America. France played a large part in the war. The French government under King Louis XVI and Queen Marie Antoinette sympathized and quietly aided the American cause while debating whether to openly join the fray. Some French soldiers of fortune even came to the colonies to fight against the hated English. One French soldier's name stands apart from all the rest.

*   *   *

Two men stood toward the center of the room and grasped hands warmly. There was twenty-five years' difference in their ages, and an ocean between the birthplace of each. They had different native languages. The Frenchman had just begun to study English on the voyage over to America. He would be fluent within a year. Perhaps the older gentleman saw in the Frenchman a younger picture of himself. They were both born leaders with a desire to make a difference. Washington had been a soldier during the French and Indian War. He had shown bravery and leadership, and his new country had selected him to carry the burdens of being commander-in-chief against the mightiest army in the world. His wilderness war experience had equipped him to wage the type of war that the British Army was not accustomed to fight.

The Marquis de Lafayette, although only nineteen, had been training to be a soldier before he was a teenager. His was a wealthy aristocratic family who had been accustomed to sending its young men to war. At the tender age of thirteen, Lafayette had been commissioned an officer in the French Musketeers. He had come to America against his family's wishes to fight in this war. It may have been dreams of glory or the desire to frustrate the hated English that prompted this venture. Lafayette would be commissioned by Congress a major general on July 31, 1777. At the time, it was thought to be a symbolic gesture to please the French nation. However, the young man took responsibilities in the war very seriously. He was born to be a soldier. In any event, a bond was formed between Washington and Lafayette that the fledgling nation would draw from.

"Your Excellency, my poor command of your language stops me from giving you an adequate greeting," Lafayette said as he grasped the hand of the commander-in-chief.

"Your manners are not lacking, my dear sir. It is a pleasure to make your acquaintance. Your English is already much better than my French. What are your plans while you are visiting our country? How long will you be staying?"

"My plans are to stay as long as I can be of service to you, sir."

The handshake continued. "I understand that you are a French nobleman, sir. In what ways do you wish to be of service?"

"Oui, Monsieur. I am a nobleman, but I am more than that. I am a soldier. I wish to serve you in your army. I will follow your command wherever it may lead. My sword is now your sword."

The smile on Washington's face was not caused by doubt in the young man's sincerity or ability. The general smiled because he could sense the beginning of a lasting relationship. Lafayette would go on to tour the troops with Washington at Valley Forge and later distinguish himself in battle at Brandywine, Rhode Island, and Yorktown.

The French were very interested in what was happening in the colonies. For centuries the French and English had been at odds. They often fought both on and off the battlefield in their own wars of culture and ideas. Only fourteen years earlier, the Americans had sided with the English against the French in war. A treaty had been signed in Paris, but hostilities remained beneath the surface. French sympathies were not necessarily *for* the colonists as much as they were *against* the British. Lafayette was one of many soldiers who volunteered to fight on the American side. He was, however, the most distinguished of the French. After their initial meeting Washington welcomed the talented Frenchman and took him into his inner circle. He became acquainted with Alexander Hamilton and Thomas Jefferson as well.

Congress had recognized early on that help was needed to be able to stand up to the finest army and navy in the world. Great Britain was proud of the fact that the sun never set on the British empire. They were not alone. Imperial designs were held by multiple nations. France, Spain, Portugal, and even Holland entertained ideas of expansion into the New World that continued to open through exploration. Spain held onto Florida, Mexico, and

Central America while France and England were engaged in a tug of war for the rest of North America. The combined forces of England and the colonies had defeated the French and Indians, but it left a bitter taste in the mouths of the French.

Congress dispatched Benjamin Franklin to France in October, 1776 with the hope of enlisting their former foe to help throw off their current master. It was not an easy task, but Franklin was the right man for the job. He was known internationally and began to circulate in scientific and literary circles. His main assignment was not so much getting the French interested in defeating their ancient enemy. The major task was to convince the French that the war was winnable.

After forcing the British out of Boston in 1775, the scene shifted to New York, where the Continental Army was defeated and moved back into Pennsylvania. Washington's army was suffering defeat, and with desertions common and enlistments ending, the outlook was bleak. Then on Christmas Day 1776, Washington surprised his foes and won a victory in Trenton, New Jersey, after the famous crossing of the Delaware River. This was followed up with a win in Princeton as well. Now Franklin had something he could show to the French, proving that the colonists were in this fight for the long haul.

Franklin continued to lobby the French to join the American cause for independence, but the French still needed some assurance of victory. That assurance came in the second battle of Saratoga in October 1777. The British, under the command of General John Burgoyne, wanted to drive a wedge through upstate New York that would separate New England from the rest of the colonies. The American forces were commanded by General

Horatio Gates. The most enigmatic figure of the Revolution was General Benedict Arnold, who was sent by Washington to support Gates. Arnold distinguished himself in the field and was wounded in the leg for his efforts. The result was an American victory, and Burgoyne's army of almost six thousand troops surrendered their arms to the colonists.

The victory of Saratoga was what was needed to give France the impetus to join in the fray. They now believed that the colonies were determined to fight as long as necessary, and that Great Britain could be defeated. France formally recognized the colonies in March 1778. Having the French as allies gave Americans new hope for ultimate victory. The first French efforts to send military aid did not meet with any great success. Washington expected a large French fleet to come across the Atlantic and harass if not outgun the British Royal Navy stationed at New York. The expected fleet took twice as long as usual to make the trip and seemed to hesitate in engaging the British. Neither Washington nor Congress had any authority over how the French military would be engaged, and communication was woefully lacking. The French fleet returned to France without having won a major victory for the embattled colonies.

When French general Rochambeau arrived in Newport, Rhode Island, on July 11, 1780, his reception by the Americans living there was underwhelming. The British had occupied the town and left a bad impression as occupiers. The French were not initially considered liberators but simply the former enemy from a decade ago. The British had also spread rumors that the French, who ate snails and frog legs, were coming to rule over them. The British soldiers had mistreated the population by destroying property and cutting down most of the trees for firewood.

Rochambeau arrived with six thousand troops and began to build a relationship with the population. He wanted to pay for any supplies his troops might need with silver coins instead of worthless colonial dollars. He offered to rebuild homes that the British had destroyed on the condition that his troops could occupy part of the buildings. This quickly began putting the local population to work and earning an income.

The fact that Rochambeau was coming was not a secret. When he would arrive and where he would land and set up headquarters no one knew. It wasn't long before the British as well as the colonists were preparing to meet the French. Washington was hoping for better results this time and was making efforts to communicate with Rochambeau. The British, of course, had other goals.

*　　　*　　　*

"Major Andre, why are you in such a hurry this day? Do you not have a few moments to spare for one of your loyal citizens?"

"Ah Sarah, I will always have time for you and your sister. Shall we step into Rivington's for a cup of tea or coffee?"

"I believe it will have to be coffee since tea is in short supply these days." She took his arm, and they stepped through the door of the coffeehouse.

"It seems the entire city is bustling with excitement today. I see Redcoats everywhere. What can be the meaning of this?"

"Well, my dear, you are correct to observe that there is news afoot. The mission is of most importance, and the town crier should not proclaim the objective of it." He leaned closer to his companion and whispered, "I am sure I can trust to your discretion."

She turned a little red and slightly opened her mouth to show surprise that he might doubt her trustworthiness. "If you can't trust me, Major, then whom can you trust?"

"True enough, my dear. True enough. We are after the bloody French today. Yes, the bloody French."

"Upon my word, Major, the French? Are they in New York?"

"No, they are not and never shall be. But they are close by. You might say they are within striking distance. What I mean by that is that *we* may strike *them*."

"Ah, now I begin to comprehend, Major. So you have your marching orders and if not New York itself, where might you be going? It's a long way to Paris, I believe."

"Yes, my dear girl, but the French have saved us the trouble of going there. The French general Rochambeau has sailed all the way to Newport, Rhode Island."

The girl gasped, "No, sir. Do not tell me they are that close, sir! Next we will see the French flag flying in the Sound itself."

"Don't despair, my dear. The danger is not yours but theirs. We are going to surprise them with a jolly good thrashing. They will soon learn what it means to face the greatest navy and army in the world."

"Oh, Major Andre, I can't help but trust in your word."

"Well, I must be going now. We can't keep Rochambeau waiting, can we?" He gave her a wink and, putting on his hat, stepped quickly through the front door.

Sarah waited a minute longer and then turned her eyes in the direction of Robert. He caught her glance and walked past the window to make sure the major had left the area. "Can I get you some more coffee, miss?"

"Yes, of course you can." Then in a quieter voice she said, "Did you hear what the major had to say?"

"I never listen to the conversations, miss." The look he gave her said otherwise and showed that he was very interested in what she had to say.

"It appears the troops are going to be busy tonight. Rochambeau is in Newport."

Robert looked at the other customers across the room. They were far enough away so as not to be heard.

"I understand, miss, and I thank you." For a few moments they looked into each other's eyes, and then she smiled and turned toward her coffee mug.

To Robert she was not only beautiful but had a depth of character that was seldom seen in one so lovely. He caught himself staring and then turned to go. He had work that needed to be done. He was now the bearer of tidings. General Washington must be informed.

19
A Day at the Fair

Going on a trip with Gramps always fed my imagination. He considered time together a learning experience, and don't get me wrong, I like to learn. To me having fun was the best way to learn, and Gramps knew how to make that happen. We had taken in a lot of history, and I had a greater appreciation of the part spies in New York played in the Revolution. Now I knew it was time to prod for a little break.

"You promised we could go to the fair on the way back, Gramps."

"I most certainly did not promise. I learned a long time ago not to make promises because all too often circumstances happen that prevent us from keeping them. However, I have every intention of stopping at the fair we saw. It's coming up in about twenty miles, so if you can hold your horses that long then we can scratch that itch." Gramps checked his mirror and noticed a dark SUV only a few car lengths behind.

"That SUV looks like the same one I saw back on Long Island."

"Really, Gramps? Maybe it's following us." I couldn't begin to disguise my excitement.

"Don't be silly, kiddo. You have been reading too many cloak-and-dagger mysteries."

"Come on, Gramps. Don't you feel like we are in a real mystery right now? We found a secret trunk that two men tried to steal from us. Then we found items in the box from the time of George Washington. Isn't that rather mysterious? Now we are tracking down who the original owner of the box was, and he may very well have been a spy from the Revolution. I would call all that a mystery, wouldn't you?"

"It makes me think that we really need a break from all this sleuthing. Going to the fair sounds like the perfect cure for what ails us."

"Yippee and sufferin' sassafrass! Now we are on the same page. Can we ride on the Blitzer roller coaster?"

"We shall see, my dear. We shall see." Gramps moved into the right lane in order to exit. A few minutes later we were standing in line to get tickets. Gramps mentioned the cost of entrance only once and concluded that it was worth it.

"What shall we do first, Gramps? Food or frolic?"

"Well, since it is now 1:00 in the afternoon, I would say food, and my nose seems to be leading me in the right direction." He pointed to a row of booths with pictures of large hot dogs, pizzas, and pretzels advertising their specialty. "What do you say to a pulled-pork sandwich?"

"I would say howdy and down the hatch. Then lets go to the Fun Zone afterward."

With the taste of tangy barbecue sauce still on our palates we entered the carnival play area. The giant Ferris wheel was the center of the attractions.

"Let's do the Ferris wheel first so we can get a bird's-eye view of the whole place," I suggested.

We got in a relatively short line to wait our turn. After about five minutes, we boarded a car and slowly moved forward as other two-seaters were loaded. Then when most of the cars were filled, the wheel began to rotate. The top was some 215 feet above the ground.

"Did you know that the tallest Ferris wheel is over 500 feet?" asked Gramps.

"No, I didn't, but it doesn't surprise me that you did. I think you should go on one of those trivia game shows, Gramps. I am sure you could win bookoo bucks."

"I will take that as a compliment although being a fountain of trivia knowledge is not one of my goals in life. I also have to give full disclosure by admitting that I looked up fairs while we were at Professor Kim's house. Do you see another ride you want to go on from up here?"

"I sure do. I want to go in the fun house with lots of mirrors, and I for sure want to ride on the Blitzer roller coaster."

"I vote yes on the fun house, but I think I will pass on the Blitzer. I want that pulled-pork sandwich to stay right where I put it. I think I will wander over to housewares while you ride that. You have your phone with you, don't you?"

"Yes, of course I do. Maybe we can meet up and go to the shooting gallery. I bet I can outscore you with a bow and arrow since Dad has been giving me lessons."

"You are on, Pocahontas, and the loser will have to do dishes when we get home." With that we took in the fun house. We couldn't help laughing at how fat or skinny we were. Every place we looked our features were distorted.

"Okay," Gramps finally said. "I am heading to housewares. We can meet in about forty-five minutes to an hour." He turned and walked swiftly while studying his map to make sure of his direction.

I watched him go and hoped he didn't run into anything. Then I headed in the direction of the Blitzer. There's no telling why I like fast rides like the Blitzer. Sometimes they make me nauseous. I thought it must be because getting scared was such a rare occurrence in my life that I liked the novelty. This particular ride wound around at high speed and then did a series of jumps. I thought I must have left my stomach back on the bench. I began to wonder what it would take for the pulled-pork to see the light of day again.

After the ride my legs felt like they were wobbling a little. I headed toward a nearby bench and then I saw him. He was across the midway in a brown suit and sunglasses. It was the same man I had seen at the gas station a few days ago. Once again he looked and acted out of place. What was a man doing by himself at the fair wearing a suit in the hot sun? The sunglasses seemed appropriate this time, but the suit did not. Being alone at the fair seemed odd, too. Then again, Gramps must be alone right now and of course I was alone. Suddenly, that very thought sent a chill up my spine. I was alone. There were many people around, but I now felt very alone with a strange man in a brown suit following me.

Getting up from the bench, I started walking down the midway. I went to the corner booth where rings were being tossed. I pretended to watch other people playing the game. My head turned only slightly, and out of the corner of my eye I saw him again. He was looking at some trinkets that were being used for prizes. I moved to the far side of the booth where there was an alley. It was dark in the alleyway, and I decided to make a break for it. I began to run. Then steps came pounding behind me. "Wait, miss!" I heard him call. I knew it must be the man in the brown suit. I kept running. The ground was uneven and my balance was off so I stumbled. "Miss," shouted the man. My knee banged on the ground and the pain hurt like the dickens. I was sure the man was running toward me. I must call Gramps. I reached for my phone to speed dial Gramps, but it wasn't there. I must have dropped it. The man in the brown suit was now standing over me and gasping for air. He reached his hand out toward me and I screamed — "aaaaaaiiiiiiiieeeeeeeeee."

"I'm sorry, miss. I must have given you a fright. Are you all right? You took a real fall. I had to catch up to you because you dropped your phone back there."

Just then Gramps appeared. "Greta, are you all right?" he asked with a calm assuring voice.

"My knee hurts a little, but I don't think I broke anything."

Gramps looked at the stranger as if to ask who he might be.

"Hi, Mr. Webb. I am Donny Dolittle at your service. Your granddaughter dropped her phone so I ran after her to return it."

Both Gramps and I were speechless and stared at the man for a few moments. Then Gramps took control.

"Let me help you up, kiddo. Now Mr. Dolittle, it appears that you have an advantage over us. You seem to be familiar with us, but we aren't sure why."

"Yes, that's true, Mr. Webb. There are some very unusual circumstances that have led to this meeting. I can explain, but perhaps we should go to a table and have some cider."

"Okay, that's fair enough. Pardon the pun."

In a few minutes the three of us were sitting at a picnic table drinking hot cider.

I blurted out, "Have you been following us, Mr. Dolittle?"

"Yes, I must confess that. I have been following you since your visit to Mrs. Sadie Woodruff. You see, I'm a private detective."

"You were watching us at the gas station, weren't you?" I asked.

"Yes, that's true. You see, Earle and John Henry Brubaker hired me to find out what was in the trunk. They think it contains something very valuable."

"And what have you found out so far?" queried Gramps.

"So far I have found it to be very fascinating but not necessarily valuable. Oh, it might be worth a few hundred dollars or even a few thousand as historical items, but not as much as Earle and John Henry were hoping."

"Have we been helping you with your discoveries?"

"Let's just say we have been working on the same thing in parallel. I have learned some things about you and your family, and I hope that doesn't alarm you. I don't think even Earle and John Henry meant to cause you grief. They just view themselves as Sadie's only surviving relatives and don't want her to squander the family wealth."

"That's ridiculous," I chimed in. "It's all her stuff, and she should be able to do what she wants with it."

"Well, the gentlemen do have certain rights as the nearest relatives, and if they can prove that she is incompetent to manage her affairs...."

I jumped to my feet. "They can't do that! She has more wits about her than two men who burglarized our home."

Gramps reached gently to my shoulder, "Please sit down, Greta. What my granddaughter is saying is very true, Mr. Dolittle. We had a fascinating conversation with Sadie and although she is indeed feisty, it does not appear she is suffering from dementia. Giving away an old trunk that she has never been able to open does not demonstrate incompetence. Neither does being reluctant to pass on her assets to nephews who have shown her very little attention. The actions of her nephews do not appear to be the most respectable or even, shall we say, competent."

"We don't need to debate that point, Mr. Webb. I was hired to find out if what the box had in it was valuable or not. I am not out to discredit the lady. Personally, I like her, as I believe you do too."

"So what do the nephews think would be valuable in the box?"

"They are not sure, but the biggest clue is Robert Townsend himself. My research has uncovered that he was a distant relative of Sadie and the nephews. In many ways he was a loner. You might even say he was an odd duck. He never married. He took care of his housekeeper's son. Some said the boy was his illegitimate son. There are many reasons to doubt that. From what I know of Townsend, he would have married his housekeeper if that had been the case. In all probability, the boy was fathered by Townsend's more outgoing brother William. But, in answer to your question, the nephews believe Townsend may have been rewarded for his espionage service and just tucked his reward away."

"We didn't find any gold doubloons or jewels in the box. I can tell you that," I piped in.

"No, you didn't, miss, and nothing else that should motivate the nephews to try to steal it. The copy of *Common Sense* and clippings from Rivington's *Royal Gazette* are great finds but not worth enough on the open market to cause this commotion."

"So why are you sharing all this with us, Mr. Dolittle?"

"I realized that Greta felt that she was being followed, and I try not to be a cause of concern for people like you. You are innocent parties to this investigation. I believe my assignment is now completed, and I will be reporting back to the nephews what I have found. I can't vouch for what further action Earle and John Henry might take, but I doubt that I will be involved. I want you to understand, Mr. Webb, in my work I often have to deal with people and situations that are not pleasant." The detective hesitated for a moment. "What I am trying to say is, I apologize if I caused you or your granddaughter concern. Also, I believe you are trying to help Sadie not help yourselves to some hidden treasure."

"For my part, Mr. Dolittle, I appreciate your having opened up to us. Now we don't have to be looking over our shoulder wondering about the dark SUV or the man in the brown suit."

"I think it's kind of cool to be followed by a detective. You're not such a bad guy. I'm a little embarrassed that I ran."

"Thank you, young lady. Mr. Webb, I will bid you goodbye. Perhaps we shall meet again, but I will not be following you."

20
Secrets in the Sea

Colorful characters fought in the rank and file of the Revolutionary War. Men like Mad Anthony Wayne and Benedict Arnold were known for their bravery and audacity. As Greta and I studied the American Revolution we discovered the first member of the Culper spy ring was one such man. Caleb Brewster had sent a letter to General Washington volunteering his services. Caleb was a known Patriot. He did not bother to hide his loyalty to the cause of independence. His was the stuff legends were made of.

* * *

The oars cut through the water at an even rate. A light fog made for a very limited visibility. Caleb Brewster had covered the passage hundreds of times. He squinted through the fog and laughed at the thought of his objective. He considered himself as a strong and brave man, yet here he was looking for laundry on a line. Victory or defeat could be determined by what garments were hanging on it. What colors were visible on the line? Was there a dark sheet at the far end? Then there it was. Yes, a dark sheet hung at the far end and it was followed by four white garments and then a gray one. That meant that a drop had been made, and he had a package waiting for him at the fifth drop point. He smiled and looked at his four-man crew. It was time to turn the boat back out to harbor.

"Well boys, it looks like our efforts have not been in vain. Pull boys! Pull!" Brewster leaned the rudder toward the harbor.

"What do you think it is this time, Caleb?" one of the crew asked.

"It's impossible to tell, Seth. It might just be a cake recipe or a lover's letter. I don't open the packages. Even if I did, I could not know what they were about."

"And why might that be, Caleb?"

"Why, it's written in code, Seth. I cannot know what the code means and neither would you. I do know that the one we delivered a fortnight ago contained information about how the British were counterfeiting our colonial dollars. That note was worth a slab of beef or I'll be keelhauled."

Brewster smiled at this again. He knew full well that the note was not only written in code, but it used an invisible ink that could not be seen unless a reagent was applied. He knew this, but it could not be told to his crew. The more people who knew about the ink, the more likely the procedure would be compromised. Brewster liked to talk about the dangers they all faced, but he also knew that some secrets must be kept.

Lemuel then spoke up. "Caleb, what's so important about counterfeiting? The British have been doing that for many months."

"True enough, Lemuel, but this was very different. They not only had a perfect likeness to Continental dollars but the very paper they used was the same that Congress used to print Continental dollars."

"So why does that make a difference?"

"Come now, Lem. Think about it. If the dollars look the same but feel different, you can tell the real dollars from the counterfeit. However, if they look the same and feel the same, then they are the same. The British were passing them out like sardines."

"Ah, now I see, Caleb. One day I might have ten dollars and then a hundred dollars or even a thousand. Milk may cost a dollar today and a thousand tomorrow. We could pile this boat full to the gunwales with Continental dollars and it wouldn't be worth a ha-penny."

"That's right, my friend. It's a very old truth. When we go a-whaling and fill our holds with oil, we can be the first to come to shore and sell for bags of gold. On the other hand, if a hundred ships come back with oil, then the price sinks. The more oil the lower the price. The more paper dollars, the less you can buy with them."

"Can you answer me this, Caleb? Whose laundry are we so interested in?" Silas asked his question with a laugh. All the crew saw the mirth of looking at laundry lines.

Caleb paused for a few moments before answering. He trusted these men with his life. They had been through skirmishes together. They had risked their lives and livelihoods to do black-market trading, and they had been together since boyhood. "'Tis the laundry of one fine lady that we have come to observe, Silas. The laundry of Anna Strong hangs on that line, lads. She be the wife of Selah Strong whom you may have heard tell."

"He's a prisoner of the Redcoats, is he not?" asked Lemuel.

"Aye, he is indeed, and you know the fate of those poor souls who go to a British prison ship. No one can force the sea to give up its secrets. Just row near a prison ship late at night and chances are you will hear a loud splash or two." The men were silent for a few moments.

"What meanest ye, Caleb? What causest the water to sound so loud?" Seth questioned. "It can't be a fish can it?"

Caleb paused a half minute and said, "Be ye witless, lad? 'Tis no fish. 'Tis what once was a man. 'Tis once was a man who sat by his hearth and bounced his child upon his knee." Lemuel let out a whistle and then Caleb continued. "Selah Strong is now on a prison ship, or he has been put to rest along with many others. Only Providence knows for sure."

The men continued to row in a somber mood through the early morning fog.

"Hush, my lads. What's that sound?" All was quiet as the men paused their oars to listen.

"'Tis nothing but the lapping of the waves, Caleb." Still they held their oars and strained to listen.

"Look yonder way, lads. What do you see?"

"I see nothing in this fog. 'Tis thicker than the morning gruel I had in me bowl, and I hear nothing but the lapping of the waves upon the water."

A minute went by and then Caleb exclaimed softly, "Yonder, lads, yonder be a light." He turned the helm away perpendicular to the light that could barely be seen in the fog. His voice was just above a whisper. "Pull now, lads. 'Tis the king's craft. Perhaps they can't see us now. Pull with all yer might and do it softly so as not to wake one newly born. If this fog holds, we may yet be undiscovered."

The four oarsmen strained their muscles with strong steady strokes as their vessel picked up speed. The faint light continued on its course. No one spoke as they knew the sound would carry along the water and betray them to the danger. The light passed near to where their course had been. Then ever so slowly, the light began to fade. The danger was subsiding.

Seth was the first to speak. "We could have taken them, Caleb. The five of us could take any boat in the water our size."

"Perhaps so, Seth, but this is not the day for us to do battle. We come on a mission, lest ye forget. We have a message to pick up and deliver. General Washington himself is waiting to hear from us."

"Oh posh, Caleb. Do ye really think the general himself reads these messages?"

"Aye, lads. Dinna doubt it. Washington is in the hills like an eagle waiting to swoop down on a mouse. General Howe is the mouse and he may be riding high now, but his time will end. These notes may seem a trifle compared to the risks we take, but they can sway a battle and win a war."

*   *   *

An hour later Brewster stood a hundred yards from the rendezvous point and watched as Abraham Woodhull rode up on horseback and dismounted. Brewster then circled around to a vantage point so he could have a clear view of the path traveled to make sure Woodhull was not followed. Normally, Woodhull would place a package underneath a log and go on his way, but for some reason the farmer appeared to be waiting to speak to him. When Brewster felt confident that no other eyes were on them, he stepped out to meet his friend.

"Abraham, it is good to see ye, but why do you tarry so?"

"Ah, Caleb, 'tis urgent business, it is. You must carry this package across and then ride like the wind to the general himself. Don't wait for Tallmadge. Washington must have this news immediately." Brewster paused only a moment as the urgency set in and then, taking the package in hand, set off at a run.

"Take care, friend," cried Brewster over his shoulder.

"Godspeed you," Woodhull called after him.

Brewster ran quickly for a quarter of a mile and then began to jog. He was a strong man and a good runner, but his boat was perhaps two miles away. This was indeed unusual to be commissioned to bypass Tallmadge and go straight to Washington's camp. He did not doubt the urgency. Usually a message could take as much as a week to get to Washington. The general often hinted that greater speed would give more value to the news it contained. Despite the general's desire for speed, however, safety was a prime consideration. If the members of the spy ring were observed making haste to deliver goods or letters, it would arouse suspicion.

Brewster wasn't sure who the city contact was. He knew Austin Roe would carry a message to Woodhull, who would tell Anna Strong where the package would be left. She would signal through her clothesline communication for Brewster to pick it up. Then his job was to cross the Sound without attracting attention and give the package to Tallmadge, who would put it in Washington's hands. For him to bypass Tallmadge and make his way to Washington's camp, the message must be of the highest value and urgency.

As he ran, Caleb wondered if Washington was still in Morristown, New Jersey. The last he had heard, the general's headquarters was at Jacob Ford's Mansion. He would go there as fast as he could, and if the headquarters had moved, perhaps they could direct him.

He had heard rumors about the French fleet being expected and believed the news must be of them. Benjamin Franklin had secured an official alliance with France in 1778, but early French endeavors had proved ineffective. Now, it was not a secret that a French fleet had sailed from France on April 6 with six thousand troops under the command of Count Jean-Baptiste Rochambeau. The real question was exactly when and where the French would land. Brewster's excitement spurred him on, and he once again picked up speed. In ten more minutes he would reach his boat and recross the Sound. Then his brown mare would take him to the general himself. What a glorious day this was to be!

21

Detective Donny Dolittle

My imagination could construct a detective much like Humphrey Bogart in an old movie. Bogart played detective Sam Spade in the *Maltese Falcon*. It was a classic black-and-white movie. Black-and-white flicks could be downright funny. Sometimes mom and dad would show us kids a black-and-white on one of our family nights and we had a ball. Plenty of popcorn flowed, and we laughed at the way technology was back in those days.

I had never met a real live detective, though. Donny Dolittle was a nice guy. He leveled with us that he had been investigating us. It made me wonder about Earle and John Henry, though. It must take a lot of gall to have someone investigated. Why didn't they just go to Aunt Sadie and talk to her about the trunk? Why not just be open and honest about what you are interested in? I think Aunt Sadie would have been nice to them about the whole thing. Okay, she would have bitten their heads off first, but then she would have been nice and they would be acting like a family again.

I guess they wanted to get what Aunt Sadie had without getting her permission. What kind of men would take something valuable from someone like Aunt Sadie? It just doesn't make any sense.

*   *   *

Detective Dolittle pulled his SUV into the driveway and turned off the motor. He let out a small sigh. His line of work called for him to meet with people who had problems. Sometimes these people were being intimidated or taken advantage of by others. He enjoyed helping those people stand up to the ones who were causing them grief. In this case, however, he was getting a bad feeling. He stepped out of the car and marched to the front door and rang the bell. John Henry opened the door.

"It's about time you got here, Dolittle. Come on in. My brother is in the other room." They walked through to the living room area where Earle was expecting him.

"Hello, Dolittle. We were expecting you yesterday."

"Sorry, gentlemen. Sometimes these things take time to put the puzzle pieces together."

"No more excuses, Dolittle. What have you got for us?" Earle demanded.

"Well, I tailed Mr. Webb and his granddaughter for the past several days. I had a good idea of where they were going, though. Your suspicions were correct that they went to the Long Island area. They visited with a friend who was a retired professor of history, and then they went to Oyster Bay and Setauket. The connection with Townsend is pretty obvious. The trunk appears to have belonged to him before it was passed on and eventually wound up in the hands of your aunt."

"What can you tell us about Townsend?"

"He was from a fairly wealthy aristocratic family. His father had a thriving trading company with several ships, but the war impacted his business. The British occupied his home during the war. It was not discovered until the early 1900s by handwriting comparison that Robert Townsend was a member of Washington's Culper spy ring. He was always referred to as Culper junior while Abraham Woodhull was Culper senior. It seems that Washington had promised to reward Woodhull and Townsend for the risks that they took, but he never did. He even felt reluctant to reimburse them for their expenses."

"We hired you to find out what we don't know, Dolittle, not what we already know. It's obvious that Townsend must have been given a big reward that was never found or passed on. That trunk must have something of value in it, and we want to know what it is."

"According to Mr. Webb, that trunk had some minor Revolutionary War trinkets. It had some clothing, a couple of books including a Bible and a copy of Thomas Paine's *Common Sense*. It had some old letters and a journal. It's all fascinating stuff but nothing of real value that you could market for more than a couple of thousand bucks."

"Then Webb is lying," Earle stated emphatically. "He has found something, and he is going to cash in. It sounds like you talked to him personally."

"Yes, I did, and I don't believe Mr. Webb is the kind of man who would lie about this."

"Nonsense, Dolittle. Every man has his price, and if I am right that trunk could be worth millions." Earle seemed very sure of this assertion.

"What makes you think it is so valuable?"

"Sadie got the trunk from her Uncle Ebenezer. The old coot had a son named Adam whom I saw two years ago. He was in poor health at the time, and I went to see him to pay my respects. His wife had died already and he had no children, so I was thinking he might want to pass some things on to his family. I wanted to find out if he had me in his will. You know how it is."

"Yes, I believe I do."

"He told me that when he was a boy he had played in the trunk and found some surprising items including something he thought might be valuable. When he played with it, he lost the key so he was afraid to tell his father about it. Years later, Eb gave the trunk to Sadie and her husband for helping him move. I don't think she ever opened it. When Adam died last year, I started asking Sadie about the trunk, and I think she got rid of it just to spite me."

"Hard to imagine."

"Webb is lying about what's in that trunk, and I want it."

"There's not a whole lot that can be done outside of offering to buy the trunk or stealing it." The detective said this as a joke, but one look at the brothers showed him they were interested in the latter idea. "No, gentlemen, I don't break laws in my line of work, and from what I understand, you already tried that option. I suspect Mr. Webb would be prepared to meet you this time, so I would strongly suggest you not try it again."

"Keep your suggestions to yourself, Dolittle. There is something else we would have you to do."

"And what would that be?"

"Sadie is in her eighties now, and we have reasons to believe that she is suffering from dementia. We want you to look into her activities to come up with times and places that she has been acting peculiar. Pictures would also help. If you can get pictures about odd things she is doing or odd ways she is dressing, then we could build a case. We also want to know how much she is worth. I suspect she is worth somewhere in the neighborhood of $2 million, but I would like to know for sure. That lawyer of hers won't divulge any information. You know how tight-lipped lawyers can be. Her accountant is even worse. You would think they should realize that when she passes away they will have to deal with us, so they should cooperate now."

"In what ways has she been acting peculiar? Can you give me some examples?"

"Giving away a valuable trunk without knowing what's in it should be enough right there. Who in their right mind does that?" Earle stated other characteristics he thought peculiar. "Her house hasn't been painted in at least ten years. All the furniture in the house is antique. Sure, the furniture is cleaned and cared for, but you have to credit that girl who helps her with that. The way Sadie dresses is very odd. I think she buys all her clothing from a secondhand store. Then there's the fact she doesn't return our calls. I have been trying to go over and visit her, so I call and that helper of hers says she is busy. How busy can an eighty-year-old lady be? She acts like she is the CEO of a major corporation and can't take the time to see her nephews."

"When did she start this behavior? When did she stop seeing you?"

"Well, she quit calling us over ten years ago. Then when we tried calling her this year, she didn't act like she wanted to see us. Then when we went to see her to ask about the trunk, she practically threw us out of the house. She threatened to call the police on us. Can you believe that? Calling the police on your own nephews?"

"Hard to imagine," the detective commented sarcastically. The brothers didn't seem to notice. "Suppose you are able to show that she is incompetent. What would you do with Mrs. Woodruff?"

"Not that it is any business of yours, Dolittle, but we would take care of her. There are plenty of facilities that we can put her in."

"We would just have to find one that isn't expensive. You know how much the costs are for one of those," John Henry added.

"That should be enough information to get you started, Dolittle. Call us in a couple of days," Earle said while ignoring his brother's comment.

"Not so fast, Mr. Brubaker. There is a little matter about my bill. I sent it to you last week but have not gotten a response."

"When we get that trunk, we will pay your bill, and you might even get a little bonus for your troubles," Earle promised.

"Mr. Brubaker, you are banking on hearsay of what a little boy thinks he saw about sixty years ago. I don't think I can take that to the bank."

John Henry spoke up again. "Listen, you little weasel, we expect you to come up with the goods before we pay you, not after."

"Easy, John. We can give Mr. Dolittle another check now in good faith. He has been helpful."

Earle scooted his roll chair over to the desk and pulled out his checkbook. He scribbled on the next check, then tore it out of the book and handed it to the detective.

"So you have your work cut out for you, Dolittle. Find out more specifically what is valuable in the trunk. Then get some evidence for us about Sadie's peculiar actions and way of dressing. Finally, if you can get a copy of Sadie's will, that would be helpful as well."

The detective left the house and climbed into his SUV. After a half hour with Earle and John Henry, he felt like he needed a long, hot shower. He had dealt with unscrupulous characters before, but not quite like this. These men seemed to think of themselves as deserving to take what was in the possession of others. Even their own aunt was fair game to them. It grated on the detective. It wasn't illegal, but it was distasteful. Yes, he needed a long, hot shower. He had a strong urge to drop the Brubakers as clients. He also knew that if he stayed on the case he might be able to help Mrs. Woodruff in some way. Right now, his shower was calling him.

*   *   *

Sadie stared at the picture and a flood of memories poured over her. Horace had been gone for twenty years, but there were times that she still felt his presence. In fact, she must have worried Marguerite when she spoke to Horace as she was prone to do.

"What do you think of all this fuss, Horace? I bet you are laughing your head off at those two nephews of yours. I say 'yours' since I don't really want to claim them. I remember when they were just kids I actually liked them. Earle was a mean little thing then but even he could do something nice. I remember once he picked a dandelion and brought it to me. Then he threw a tantrum because the fuzz had flown off. I think he was about eight years old then. John Henry was a sweet boy, but he couldn't seem to think for himself. He just did what Earle told him to do."

"Why are they so interested in Uncle Ebenezer's trunk? That old thing has been in the attic for years." Once again she looked at the picture of her husband and a tear trickled down her cheek. "I wish you were here, Horace. You always seemed to know what to do in situations like this. Those boys always liked you. They lived down the street and would come over and you played football with them. You always seemed to have time for the neighborhood kids, too. I am still mad at you, Horace. You should not have left me like you did. I know you couldn't help it. Your heart gave out."

Sadie leaned over and opened one of the small jewelry boxes on the table. She began to move items around until she found what she was looking for.

"Yes, I think that's it." She lifted a small key from the box. "I think that's the one. I can't be sure. It's been there for so long." Her fingers lowered the box lid and then reached out to the picture again. "I will give the key to that Greta girl. She and her grandfather seem to get along pretty well. I wish I had a granddaughter now, like her. You must be wishing we had children, so I wouldn't have to be alone now. Don't worry, dear. I am not really alone. I still like talking to you even though you don't say much. Then again, you were never much of a talker. But maybe it was because I did so much talking you couldn't get a word in edgewise. I wish I had let you talk more. I wish I could hear you now. No matter. The Good Lord left me here and took you. Yes, they have the trunk now. I think you're right. They should have the key, too."

"I hope to join you soon, Horace, but right now there is work to do." She closed the box and slipped the key into her apron pocket. She motored her chair toward the door.

22

Love and War

Greta and I had become fascinated with the complexity of the American Revolutionary War. It was more than just death and destruction. It was filled with noble deeds as well as simple acts of kindness. There was also romance. Even a war can't put a hold on all the affairs of the heart. One of the main characters of the Revolution courted a young lady that led to marriage and eventually affected the outcome of the war.

Benedict Arnold married Philadelphia socialite Peggy Shippen on April 8, 1779. She was from a well-known Loyalist family, which added to Philadelphia's discontent with General Arnold's administration. Arnold had been appointed the colonists' military commander in Philadelphia, and he had proven to be a very unpopular choice. In particular, James Reed, who was president of the Pennsylvania council, was pressuring Arnold to explain actions he had taken that seemed to be self-serving. This eventually led to a military court-martial. Arnold was acquitted at the court-martial of all but two minor charges. He was left with a bitter taste about his dealings with the Pennsylvania politicians. He also suffered physically from his wounds at Saratoga that resulted in a continuing limp and hampered his effectiveness as a field commander.

*　　　*　　　*

Edward Shippen gazed at his daughter as if she were a stranger. "I am most distressed about your alliance with General Arnold, my dear. Ever since the wedding I have had many sleepless nights. I am afraid that your marriage has irreparably injured our standing with the Crown. We wanted to be neutral, but now that seems impossible."

Peggy Shippen Arnold was a very pretty young wife with a tender complexion and gray-blue eyes. Hers was a world of contradiction. She could enthrall and entertain on the dance floor or spend a quiet evening with her father reading in the library. "Oh Papa, Benedict is my very dear husband, and he thinks the world of you, and I thought you returned his esteem."

"Yes, I do. I am very fond of him, but his position gives me cause for concern. You and he are on opposite sides of this conflict. It appears that you focus exclusively on the parties and gaiety while this land is ravished by the atrocities of war. How can you reconcile the disparity between the two of you?"

"I never try to reconcile or justify my feelings, Papa. However, my feelings cannot be denied. Benedict is a very charming man, and he has shown great bravery even if he is on the other side. Besides, Papa, how do we know where these events may lead? Are we really that certain that England will win in the end? When men like Benedict and General Washington support the Patriot cause, then could it be possible that the colonists will succeed eventually?"

"Hush, my dear. You should never even suggest such an idea. These rebels cannot possibly be victorious."

"Then we must keep up our appearance of neutrality, Papa. Since the Crown will undoubtedly be victorious, we must continue to have commerce with the Loyalists. However, if the Patriots prove to hold the advantage, then my relationship with Benedict will be a great benefit to us. Besides, there are other possibilities to consider."

"What do you mean by that, Peggy? What other possibilities?" The father was searching for an out – a way of escaping from the political dilemma they appeared to be in.

"You know, Papa, that Benedict has been fully devoted to the Patriot cause. He has been General Washington's most able commander leading to victories at Ticonderoga and Saratoga."

"Yes, but that was so very long ago. Congress has forgotten his valor as well as his victories."

The daughter's eyes flashed with brilliance at her next speech. "Nevertheless, the wounds he suffered in the Patriot cause should have been recompensed. He thought his position in Philadelphia was his reward for his service, but that Mr. Reed caused problems throughout. He seemed to have a great deal of animosity toward Benedict, which led to the court-martial. Benedict was magnificent at the court-martial and refuted their accusations most soundly. I was so proud of him."

"Yes, I believe he was vindicated, my dear, but it has not aided him in recovering the fortune that he lost in serving the Patriot cause. I am of the opinion that Congress will never make up for his losses. Frankly, my dear, I don't believe that Congress has the means to recompense him the fortune he is entitled to. They have a war to manage, and because of the counterfeiting scheme they had to practically declare bankruptcy. How can they pay your husband back?"

"Oh, Papa, as you say, Congress may not have the means, but there is still an avenue that may be open." She lowered her eyes with the thought.

"My dear, whatever do you mean?" He looked intently at his daughter for an explanation. There were times when his daughter seemed a complete enigma to him. She could have chosen from among many eligible suitors for a husband. Why did she have to settle on General Arnold?

"Have you not heard, Papa, what Sir Henry Clinton has been offering to those who would come back to the side of the Crown?"

There was a long pause now as the eyes of father and daughter became fixed on one another.

"Oh, my dear, you do so concern me. Do you actually realize what you are saying? Would your husband consider such an option? It would be filled with the gravest of risks. It could be dangerous for us all."

"I am not saying, Papa, that Benedict has determined in his own mind yet what his course of action will be. I am just saying that with our coming baby our needs are very real. Our expectations of what may be received from Congress are much in doubt. My dear Benedict must consider the needs of his family in making decisions."

"Ah yes, the baby, but I must counsel you, my dear. Do not let changing circumstances press you and General Arnold into doing something rash."

"No, Papa, but changing circumstances and changing times can elicit changing attitudes and new decisions."

*　　　*　　　*

General Arnold was thirty-eight when he married eighteen-year-old Peggy. From the beginning, financial pressures weighed on the happiness of the couple. An expected baby prompted a serious discussion about the future.

"Can our situation be as dire as you make it out to be, dearest?" Peggy put her arm on her husband's sleeve.

"If anything, I have understated our situation. I have had to put our house in New Haven up for sale, but I have not had any offers on it. Our Mount Pleasant home will have to be rented out." Benedict frowned, and then added, "The Spanish ambassador has shown some interest in it."

"But dearest, even if we rent out Mount Pleasant, you do not expect that to be an answer to our financial concerns, do you? We must have a more lasting resolution."

"Yes, but what can be done? I have been speaking with General Washington to see if he can offer some redress to these difficulties. I do believe his hands are tied."

"Perhaps we should be considering a solution from another direction entirely."

"Whatever do you mean, my dear?"

"Do you remember Major John Andre? He made quite a name for himself while the British were occupying Philadelphia."

"Yes, I recall Andre. Has he been promoted to major now?"

"He has indeed, and he reports directly to Sir Henry Clinton. As I understand it, he is in charge of intelligence for General Clinton."

"What are you suggesting, my dear? What does John Andre have to do with us?"

"Precisely this, my dear. Sir Henry Clinton is offering consideration for anyone who would be willing to change allegiance to the Crown. There, I have said it. Chastise me if you will."

There was a lengthy silence following these statements. Both husband and wife drank in the magnitude of what Peggy had said. Arnold rose from his seated position and tested his injured leg. He turned his back to her and walked toward the other side of the room with a slight limp. She watched him, half expecting him to explode in response to what she had said.

At last Arnold spoke in a measured, even tone, "Do you fully realize what you are saying? I have shed blood for my country including my own. The leg that no longer supports me cries out and says 'foul.'" He turned to her and spoke with an understanding voice. "However, I must be completely honest with you, my dearest. I have already contemplated this possibility. I have been in touch with Major Andre through an intermediary. Yet I am much perplexed. Washington is the man I admire above all others. It is his esteem that keeps me on our present course. How can I lose his goodwill? I have always been a man of decision, but now I hesitate. How can I tread this path?

"Oh Benedict, my darling Benedict. You have given your blood and your health in a cause that at one time seemed right to you, and what has been your reward? You could have perished on the battlefield, but Providence spared you. Yet still you have continued to be faithful to Washington. Congress has turned its back on you. They have denied you promotion time and again. They have denied recompensing you for monetary losses. Then when given some semblance of command in Philadelphia, they attacked you as a common criminal. They slandered you openly in the papers. They called you before a court and accused you of shameless acts. And what did Washington do? He came to your defense in a most unwilling manner. He gave more deference to James Reed than to you. And still you call him friend. He does not deserve your faithfulness, nor does he deserve your friendship. Now that we are one step away from destitution, where is his friendship? When our baby is born, what will Congress do? Where will Washington's friendship get us then? I tell you, Benedict, it is more than I can bear." She broke down and began to sob with her head in her hands.

Once again he took the seat nearest her and placed his hand on her head. With a gentle caress he said, "Peace, my little lamb, peace. Our child will not live in poverty. I promise you that. Give me some time now. I must think about these matters. You can rest assured, though. You and our baby will not live in want."

*   *   *

The rider pranced his horse up to the small group of officers and saluted the general. Washington had been reviewing the troop positions along with his aides, Hamilton and Lafayette. "Your Excellency, I have been looking for you," said the rider.

"Ah, General Arnold, it is good to see you. What brings you here this morning?"

"I have been pondering our past conversations and wonder if you have decided on my future."

"Yes, Benedict, I have. We have long been appreciative of your skills. The position that I have intended is for you to command my left wing." This announcement was met by a stiff silence, which was not what Washington expected. Commanding the left wing during a battle would be a position of honor and possible glory. Arnold had distinguished himself many times under fire and seemed to thrive under duress. The offer of this post should have been met with jubilation. Arnold had requested the command of the fort at West Point, which was on the Hudson River. It was a very strategic position but a defensive post. Washington thought it would be a waste of Arnold's talents compared to a battle assignment. Now Arnold's cold response was difficult to understand. Had his wounded leg dampened the spirits of one of Washington's best field generals? A few minutes later, Arnold rode off to their headquarters to await the commander-in-chief.

Little did Washington know that Arnold had been making plans regarding West Point. During his troubles in Philadelphia, he had come to a crossroads in his life. He had come to the conclusion that the American political leaders, in spite of Washington, would never truly appreciate him. He had confided to a Philadelphia Tory named Joseph Stansbury that he would entertain an offer to change sides in the war. Stansbury had traveled to New York and spoken to the British intelligence chief, Major John Andre. Andre carried the message to General Henry Clinton. The British were all ears. They had often made overtures to the Continental Army to entice deserters. It had never occurred to them that someone as high ranking as Benedict Arnold would take them up on their offer. Secret negotiations had been taking place. Arnold was seeking to gain in prestige and, yes, monetarily. His debts had been mounting, and unless he found a solution he would be buried under them. He had piqued the British interest, but he now needed to deliver something valuable to them. He needed to take charge of a prize that the British would consider paying as much as 20,000 pounds for. Andre had suggested he take an assignment in the south that he could turn over to them. Arnold countered with the offer of West Point. Now he desperately needed to convince Washington to give him the prize.

If Arnold could turn over West Point with perhaps three thousand men, he would be striking a blow against those who had treated him so badly. With morale in the colonies at a low point, it would make a difference in this war. Both sides wanted the war to end. It was he, Benedict Arnold, who had within his person the means to bring an end to this strife. The reward of 20,000 pounds would be just the beginning. He would have the rank of general in the British Army, which was the ultimate fighting force in the world. A grateful England would undoubtedly give him a knighthood. It was almost within his grasp. Still, he needed to convince Washington.

*   *   *

Many parts of the city had been blackened with fire when the British took control. A rebuilding effort was required, it would not be completed for some time. Commerce still thrived within hubs of activity like Rivington's coffeehouse.

"I have not seen you here at Rivington's recently, Major Andre," Sarah hailed the young officer. "Whatever the king's business is must have been extremely important to keep you so occupied."

"Ah, Miss Sarah. Only the most critical of business could deprive me of the pleasure of seeing you and your sister. I trust you and your family are well?"

"Oh, they are all very well, Major, but I suspect that you have been hard at work writing another poem or making a drawing or even creating a new play to be spread abroad among your many admirers. Your success in Philadelphia is well known, Major."

"I wish my mind had been so agreeably engaged, my dear, but alas, my endeavors were required in other directions." He leaned closer to his companion and spoke very softly so as not to be overheard. "I am going on a mission soon that I believe may make a difference in the outcome of the war."

"My goodness, Major, I thought all your business made a difference in the outcome of the war. Why should this business be any different? Are you leading a regiment into battle to capture Washington himself? Now that would be a feat indeed."

The major smiled at this last comment by the lady. "You are very astute, my dear, and closer to the truth than you may have realized. The fact of the matter is that I am not at the head of a regiment but will be going alone."

Sarah gave him a winsome smile and, leaning in closer to him whispered, "You astonish me, Major. So you are going to ride into Philadelphia by yourself and breach Washington's army and capture him like any common soldier? I am only disappointed that you will not capture Congress while you are there and bring the entire lot of them back in chains."

"You should not doubt me, mademoiselle. I have more powers than you imagine. However, I will be completely honest with you by saying I may need the help of one other individual." Her eyes were now bright with wonder at what Major Andre had been suggesting. Could he really be thinking he would capture General Washington?

"I am surprised that you would need anyone's help to win this war, Major. Are you saying that General Clinton may still be useful to you after all?" she teased.

"Not at all, my dear. It is not General Clinton's help I will need. He can be useful at times, but not this time. No, the person I will get help from is a name that starts with an *A* just as mine does. I must leave you with that, my dear. I have said too much already, so I must depart before I give you all of my secrets. It has been a pleasure as always."

Andre stood and bowed to the lady before making his way to the front door. She gave a small nod to him as she kept turning the conversation over in her mind. Was Washington really in danger? Who was the man whose name began with an *A* that could do him harm? How could one man be useful to Major Andre? She tried not to look excited. It would be a mistake to look animated. She should wait a few minutes more before leaving the coffeehouse. She wished Robert were here. He might be able to figure out the clues she had just been given. It may be really nothing after all, but she didn't think so. She felt like she had some information forming in her thoughts that needed to be communicated. Oh, where was Robert? She got up very slowly so as not to arouse suspicion. She had to find him. She had to find him now.

23

Greta and Gramps Report

School was just a few weeks away, and I was having mixed emotions. The start of something like a school year always held some promise of excitement and challenges that needed to be met. Summer was a blast, though. I was excited about my parents' trip almost as much as I would have been to go along. The birth of a new cousin was a blessing that we had been anticipating for months. Spending time with Gramps was always fun, but this year it was really special.

The mystery trunk held items from history that fed my imagination. One night I dreamed I was Agent 355 back in New York City. I dressed up as a maid and snuck into General Henry Clinton's office and started going through his battle plans which were on his desk. Then suddenly the door burst open and two guards rushed in and grabbed me. I woke up just in time to avoid facing a firing squad or a hangman's noose.

I wondered if I could change my schedule to study American history this year. I also had a weird feeling that we didn't know everything about the trunk. There was something still missing.

"Greta, What do you say we pay Aunt Sadie a visit today?"

"That would be great, Gramps, but first let me make a batch of gingerbread cookies to take with us."

"Perfect, kiddo. I'll call her and give her a heads-up."

Two hours later we were traveling in the black Jeep.

"Did you mention the cookies to her?" I asked.

"Yes, and I would have to say she was very receptive."

A few minutes later we pulled into the driveway. Stepping up to the door, we punched the bell only one time. Marguerite came to the door quickly this time and let us in.

"Hello, Marguerite, how are things today?"

"Very well, Mr. Webb. Mrs. Woodruff is looking forward to seeing you." We followed her into the parlor. Aunt Sadie was in her wheelchair over near the small fire in the fireplace. It was a cool day toward the end of summer, and I think Aunt Sadie just likes fires for the sake of ambiance. She wheeled about to face us as soon as we entered. A big smile brightened her face.

"Great balls of fire, if you didn't come back. I was beginning to think I had imagined your visit before. But then again, those no-account nephews called to see if you had brought the trunk back. I told them it was none of their business. I also told them I didn't want it back 'cause I was afraid they would come over again." She laughed at this, and we weren't sure if she was kidding them or us. "Now where are those cookies you promised me?"

"Right here, Aunt Sadie," I said and held out the desired treat.

"I haven't had a gingerbread cookie in Lord knows how long. Marguerite, you better get one while you can." The young girl reached out for her cookie, and Gramps and I joined in too. Between munching we began discussing the just completed trip.

"Aunt Sadie, it was a fantabuloso trip. I had never been to Long Island, and we took the ferry while we were there. Long Island Sound is really big. Gramps wanted to go where some of the Patriots lived back in the Revolutionary War, and we did. Then on the way back we went to the county fair. Have you been to the fair, Aunt Sadie?"

"Goodness, child, take a breath and give your grandfather a chance to say something. Yes, I used to love going to the fair. It wasn't easy since I was held down by this infernal chair."

Gramps now had some questions for Aunt Sadie. "So, Mrs. Woodruff, we traced the contents of the trunk back to a possible connection with the Revolutionary War and people living on Long Island during that time. In fact, we think that the initials RT on the box may have belonged to a Robert Townsend. He was from Oyster Bay on Long Island. Do you know if you have relatives who came from Long Island and what their names were?"

"Well, I'll be switched. I recall my grandfather Eli speaking about the Townsends of Long Island. It may have been Oyster Bay, but it's been so long I can't rightly be sure about it."

"Do you recall if you were related to the Townsends who lived on Long Island?"

"Well, I can't rightly say, but it would be a good guess that I am. You see, Mr. Webb, in those days the world was a lot smaller and Long Island was a more tightly knit community. In a way, everybody was related to everybody else. At least we all knew each other and were either related or friends or enemies, hah!"

"Yes, I believe you are right about that, Mrs. Woodruff. That's why there were some folks on Long Island who could trust each other and do espionage work for the colonists."

"Espionage? Do you mean they were spies? How thrilling!"

"Yes, they were spies. Robert Townsend, Abraham Woodhull, Caleb Brewster, and Anna Strong were working together as a spy ring. Benjamin Tallmadge headed it up for General Washington."

"Washington himself? Well, I never did hear the likes of it. But that doesn't explain why Earle and John Henry care so much about that trunk. They were never very interested in history."

"No, it really doesn't. So far as we can tell, the value is just in the history of what was in the box. What we found was really amazing. There was an old family Bible, some letters, a journal, clothing, a copy of *Common Sense* by Thomas Paine, and some pages from a newspaper printed during the war called *The Royal Gazette*."

"The only thing of value you just said was the Bible, but not for the usual reasons."

Gramps smiled and said, "I know what you mean, Aunt Sadie. Actually, the Bible we found is an edition published by Robert Aitken. We did some research on this and found out that the British had forbidden Bibles to be printed in America in English. They were printed at Oxford and shipped over. Then when the war started, the Bible shipments stopped. No surprise there. Aitken received permission from Congress and printed New Testaments in 1777, 1778, 1779, and 1781. Then in 1782 Aitken printed the whole Bible. The Bible we found has historical value and there may only be about forty in existence today so it is truly rare. I doubt that your nephews knew about the Bible and I don't really understand their interest in the box. Do you have any idea why they wanted the box, Aunt Sadie?"

"No, I sure don't. Oh, I almost forgot. I have something for you that I found. I was doing some thinking this past week and remembered that I did have a key after all. Marguerite, where did I put that key?"

"I'm not sure Mrs. Woodruff. I will go check your dresser drawer. That's where you usually put important papers and things." The young girl walked out of the room for a moment and then returned empty-handed.

"It wasn't there, Mrs. Woodruff. Where else could it be?"

"Oh drat, I just forget too many things these days." Then she raised her right index finger to her temple and smiled. "Ah, of course." She reached her hand down in her apron pocket and pulled out the item in question. She handed the key to Gramps and waited for his reaction. Gramps turned the key over in his hand and I think we both felt like it was too small to actually fit the trunk. "Uncle Eb gave me that key a few years after Horace died. He said he thought it might go with the trunk. The trunk was already in the attic, and I didn't feel like going up there to give it a try, so I just put it in a drawer and forgot about it."

"We do appreciate your finding this. We will see if it fits. Thank you very much."

Gramps declined another cookie while Aunt Sadie and I each took one.

There was a lull in conversation so I spoke up. "Aunt Sadie, what do you do in your spare time?"

"Land sakes, child! At my age, all the time is spare time. In answer to your question, though, I like to have Marguerite drive me down to the rest home. Then I can go in and visit with some folks. I like to take in some John Philip Sousa marching music to play for them. There's nothing like good marching music to get the blood flowing."

"You're right about that, Aunt Sadie," I said and couldn't help smiling.

"Some people think they are religious by going to church. That's not what the Bible says, though. True religion is visiting widows and orphans, so that's what I like to do. Now don't get me wrong. I go to church too. When I am home, though, I like to watch basketball. Those players move very fast and they can turn on a dime and do some amazing tricks with the ball. Oh yes, I like watching tennis too. What about you, dearie? What do you like to do in your, uh, 'spare' time?"

"Well, I have to get my studies done first, and then I like to play sports. Watching sports is good, too, and I learn a lot from it. I am hoping to get a tennis scholarship someday, but I don't know if I am good enough."

"You never know till you try, sweetheart. You never know till you try."

"Would you like another cookie, Aunt Sadie?"

"No, I have to learn when to stop, but you can leave the rest if you've a mind to. Marguerite and I can finish them off at a later time. There's just one more thing I should mention. We have been noticing a strange car driving around here, and it looks very suspicious."

"What is suspicious about it?" questioned Gramps.

"First of all, it moves very slowly. Then it comes back an hour later. Then it comes back the next day and does the same thing. I do believe someone inside is taking pictures."

"Can you think of any reason someone would be coming to take pictures, Aunt Sadie?"

"I am not sure, but when it comes to peculiar happenings, those no-good nephews of mine could easily have a hand in it. They just always seem to be up to something."

"Gramps, do you think it could be Detective Dolittle?" I asked and turned to Aunt Sadie, "Was it a large, dark car?"

"Detective Dolittle, my stars who might he be?" she asked.

"I didn't want to mention it, Aunt Sadie, and make you worry," Gramps said. "On our trip we were followed by a detective who was hired by your nephews. At one point he politely introduced himself. I don't believe he is dangerous to any of us, but he may be investigating on behalf of your nephews."

"Then he is wasting his time and my nephews' money. Although, knowing my nephews, he will have the devil of a time getting paid by them. They throw around nickels like they were manhole covers. It serves him right, though, for coming around here and snooping on me. For the life of me, I can't imagine what they would be investigating. I don't have anything to hide. Next time I may just call the police."

"Mrs. Woodruff, I do believe I see that car parked down the street," said Marguerite.

"Land sakes, child. Call 911 this instant!"

"Mrs. Woodruff, give me a few minutes and perhaps I can straighten this out," requested Gramps. He stood and went out the door. Two minutes later Gramps was tapping on the window of the dark vehicle and a startled man inside looked up to see him. He then rolled his window down at the sight of Gramps.

"Mr. Webb, you surprised me."

"Mr. Dolittle, I must ask you why you are here. You are causing a great deal of concern on the part of the ladies inside. They were just getting ready to call the police and have you arrested. I don't think that would be in your best interests. If you have questions that you would like to ask Mrs. Woodruff, then I suggest you come inside and talk to her. She might be a little prickly, but it is better than spying on her."

The detective looked very sheepish like a five-year-old with his hand caught in the cookie jar. "Mr. Webb, I apologize. I am not sure I am ready to face Mrs. Woodruff right now, though. I did not think anyone was noticing me, but obviously I was wrong." The detective sighed. "Of course, you are right. I should apologize to Mrs. Woodruff. I will come in and do so at once. Perhaps just asking her some questions would be the best way after all." A few minutes later the detective and Gramps joined the ladies in the parlor.

"Well, young man. What have you got to say for yourself? We are not used to seeing cars on our street that don't belong here. Nor people for that matter." Sadie sized up the detective standing before her.

"Mrs. Woodruff, I sincerely apologize if I caused you any

concern. Yes, your nephews hired me to observe what is going on in this neighborhood. They want to make sure their interests are not overlooked."

"Their interests, my foot! They have no interests in what I do or why I do it. You can tell them for me that when I do something that concerns them I will let them know about it. Otherwise, they should stay away if they know what's good for them."

"Yes ma'am, I understand what you are saying. They mean you no harm. I believe they just want to take care of you."

"Spying on me is a funny way of taking care of me, don't you think? Anyways, if you want to know something about me, come to the front door and knock."

"Yes ma'am," said the extremely embarrassed detective. We talked for a few minutes more and then Detective Dolittle vacated the premises.

Aunt Sadie looked at me and said, "A Sherlock Holmes he definitely was not. I don't believe he could figure out a three-letter crossword puzzle word that started with C and ended with T and got chased by dogs."

It's too bad Detective Dolittle wasn't much help. I kept thinking there just had to be a mystery about the trunk. Something that old with all that cool stuff in it had to have a secret or two. I was starting to doubt, though. Maybe its secrets were from just too long ago for us to know any more about the trunk.

24

Spy Meets Spy

Greta and I were learning a great deal about the complex psychological makeup of General Arnold. His courage had been displayed numerous times on the battlefield while his pride had been offended just as often. His failure to respect the political authorities meant that the rewards he so yearned for would remain outside of his grasp.

Arnold was also an incurable romantic, which led to his alliance with Peggy Shippen. Now with a Loyalist wife and new baby, Arnold was torn between a Patriot cause and finding a solution to mounting debts. Small steps had been taken that ultimately led to an ugly word – betrayal.

*   *   *

Sarah walked into the shop of Templeton and Stewart where Robert Townsend was employed and was relieved to find him alone.

"Robert, I have been looking all over for you. I have just had a most enlightening conversation with Major Andre."

"Yes, I can see by your countenance that you have something sensitive to communicate. Allow me to lock the front door and put the sign out so we can discuss this privately." They quickly went over the conversation Sarah had had with Major Andre.

"First of all, we must take the threat of his capturing General Washington seriously," said the lady. "His manner was proud but not frivolous."

"I doubt that he meant kidnapping the general," Robert responded. "Washington is never really alone. He has staff constantly with him for discussion and to convey messages to others. No one man could kidnap the general."

"Then let's assume it is knowing where General Washington is and attacking at that precise time with a group of men. So Major Andre could be speaking of a high-ranking officer who reveals the whereabouts of Washington. That would be a high-ranking officer whose name starts with an *A*. Could it be a reference to Alexander Hamilton? He is Washington's most trusted aide."

"I seriously doubt that it could be Hamilton. All I know of the man speaks of the highest moral character. However, there is a man who has been in the news a great deal who may be a possibility. He has had political problems in Philadelphia and he is married to a lady from a Tory family." Robert paused now gazing at the smile on Sarah's face.

"Lest you forget, dear Robert, I am a lady from a Tory family. It is no great crime to marry such as I."

"Ah yes, my dear, but I sincerely believe that you are one of a kind." She blushed at this remark. He returned to the subject at hand. "The lady he is married to is also a good friend with Major Andre."

"I am shocked, but I do believe you are suggesting Benedict Arnold is the man who could betray General Washington."

"Yes, and it actually fits what we know. He showed great courage in battle and was wounded for his efforts. He almost lost a leg and still has trouble on horseback. As I understand it, he was recently given command of West Point. It all seems to fit. Washington often goes to visit Patriot posts. Arnold would know he would be coming to the fort and arrange for the guards and the garrison to be unprepared. The British could attack at a precise moment and capture the fort and the commander-in-chief. When Andre said it would make a difference in the war, he was grossly understating the situation."

The color drained from Sarah's face as she felt the danger of the situation. "But Robert, how can we be sure?"

"We really can't be sure, Sarah, but Washington needs to be on his guard, especially if he is to travel to West Point. Sarah, I must bring this news to him immediately. Right or wrong, Washington must be informed." They looked at each other a moment longer, and then Sarah left so Robert could hurry to pass the news.

*   *   *

Three days later a meeting took place in a small house near the edge of the Hudson River.

"We have much to discuss, Major Andre. Since my appointment as the garrison commander at West Point, I am now in a position to deliver to you what could mean the end to the war. I trust you have brought me some guarantee of my being recompensed for the risks I have been taking." The general had come to negotiate and spoke bluntly to the younger officer.

"Yes, yes, General Arnold. We are well aware of your risks. We are prepared to reward you accordingly. You will be given the rank of general in our army plus a sum commensurate with the number of men you are able to surrender to us at the appointed time. I also believe you will be rewarded far beyond that. Back in England you would be a celebrated figure as the man who brought an end to this senseless insurrection. You would probably be given a knighthood."

"A knighthood, well imagine that." Arnold smiled at hearing that his plans might well be rewarded as he had hoped. Yes, he would truly deserve to be knighted and associate with royalty. He could well imagine being received by King George himself and dining at St. James's Place.

"We are also very interested in obtaining the Big Prize when you come over. Do you have further ideas as to how we might capture Washington himself?"

"Of course, Major. If anything, I am a calculating man. As you know, General Washington often visits his troops at their outposts. In fact, I am expecting him in about a week. He usually spends several days with us and reviews the troops and fortifications."

"Are you not apprehensive about that inspection since you have been modifying the fortifications for our transfer of control?"

"Not at all, Major. It is true that Washington has a keen eye, but my plans include shifting fortifications at a precise time. All will be accomplished under cover of darkness. This will allow for a path of approach that a platoon of perhaps twenty men can take charge of the powder magazine. Resistance will be rendered all but futile."

"Yes, indeed, General, but what about Washington? How will we get him?"

"I have drawn maps of the area that I will give you. While one group of your men captures the magazine, two other groups will cut off the roads. Washington cannot escape if your men do their duty."

"Excellent, General, excellent! I can picture Washington himself being aroused wearing his nightcap and surrounded by a group of Redcoats. What a look will be on his face!" Both men threw back their heads and gave a hearty laugh at the imagined distress of the colonial commander-in-chief. Then General Arnold stopped and looked very seriously at the Redcoat officer.

"It is a good plan, Major, and it will work, but I need some assurance. If for some reason the plan fails and I have been revealed, I still need to be recompensed. There will be no turning back."

"Here is a letter from General Clinton. I believe it is the assurance you are looking for."

Arnold took the letter and studiously read through it. "Yes, I believe it is. The good General Clinton has promised that even if the plan were to fail and I were to come over, then I would be recompensed."

"I believe our business is at an end, General. You have your letters of assurance and I have the plans for the taking of West Point. Now, my only concern is getting back to my side of the Sound. The waterway appears to be guarded by a Patriot boat. I will need to return overland. Can you give me a horse and an escort?"

"I can only give you one man as a guide, but you have a pass signed by me that should get you through the Patriot lines. Once back to your side, you will need to act immediately to put our plan into action. When Washington gets here, I will have three cannons fired to signal you that the plot must take place that very night. If you can comply then you must fire three cannons an hour later, and I will know to expect you."

"Why only three cannons, General? Surely Washington deserves to have more fired in his honor."

"Yes, but the general is concerned about wasting powder. He will probably give me a scolding for firing that many. Three will be sufficient."

The two conspirators were not unfriendly as they bid each other adieu. Andre even asked Arnold to give his regards to his wife, Peggy. General Arnold returned to his headquarters at West Point while Andre began his journey back to the safety of his side. It was a passage that had proved treacherous to others before him. Andre was accompanied by Joshua Smith and his servant and spent one night along the way. When they came to Croton River Bridge, Smith bid him goodbye and Godspeed. Andre had been anxious during the journey. Dressed in civilian clothing behind enemy lines, he knew he could be taken as a spy, and that is exactly what happened.

John Paulding, Isaac Van Wart, and David Williams had been camped along the trail in the hopes of meeting travelers who could be relieved of their valuables. These three highwaymen were so-called Cowboys and considered themselves Patriots. John Paulding first stepped into the road to bar Andre from advancing.

"Stand and deliver, man. Where are ye bound?"

The first thing Andre said was true enough. "I am an officer of the king and on important business that should not be delayed. If you trouble me not, I will give you this gold watch and bid you adieu."

Paulding replied, "Are ye now? And what need have I of the time? Dismount and let us have a look at you." The three men were carefully eyeing the fine clothing worn by the traveler. The boots were of particular interest.

Now suspecting they were Patriots Andre changed his tactics. "Delay me not, gentlemen. My name is Anderson, and I have a pass from General Arnold himself, who would take it amiss if I am hindered." Andre handed them the pass. The three men began to look at it in such a way that Andre wondered if they could actually read.

Then Paulding said, "Stand over here, Mr. Anderson, and take off your boots." Paulding wanted the expensive footwear for his own. Andre hesitated and then did as he was told. He was very awkward in removing the first boot, which caused Paulding to feel his stocking.

"What have we here?" he exclaimed. "There are papers in your stockings. Take them off and let me see." Andre hesitated for a moment and the three motioned with their rifles so he obeyed. While one rifle stayed pointed at the captive, the other two looked over the papers with great interest.

"Well bless my soul, if you ain't a spy, Mr. Anderson. Now we can be truly honest with each other. What will you give us to let you go?"

Andre swallowed hard and replied, "I will give you any number of guineas you shall name to take me to the British lines."

There was stillness for perhaps thirty seconds then all three leaned back and roared with laughter. Paulding said, "Mr. Anderson, we have your watch, your horse, your saddle, and your boots. What have you bought in return? You have bought yourself an audience with Colonel Jameson. March that way, and be quick about it."

An hour later in North Castle, Colonel John Jameson found himself in a most awkward position. Three highwaymen had brought him a prisoner named Anderson who held a pass signed by General Arnold himself. The documents found on this Mr. Anderson were very incriminating, but the pass should have been honored. Jameson knew Arnold's signature very well, and now he was in a quandary as to what to do. The papers showed details of the garrison at West Point, and the prisoner had no real explanation for possessing them. He decided to send the plans to Washington himself and let him decide. As for Mr. Anderson, he would send him back to West Point. General Arnold had given him a pass, so Arnold would have to decide what to do with him.

Not far away, Benjamin Tallmadge had returned to North Castle from a scouting mission. He was advised of the capture of Mr. Anderson. He also had a note from General Arnold advising him of a Mr. Anderson who should be given an escort to come visit Arnold at West Point. This Anderson was leaving the West Point area when captured carrying details of the fort. Tallmadge had been advised by the Culper ring in the last few days that there was a big operation in the works. There was even the suggestion that Washington himself might be in danger. As the chief intelligence officer, Tallmadge did not allow for coincidence. He believed a common thread ran through these events. Tallmadge hurried over to see Colonel Jameson and explain his suspicions to him.

"Colonel, may I have a word with you?"

"Certainly, Major, what can I do for you?"

"It's your prisoner, sir. I don't believe we have an ordinary situation here. No ordinary merchant carries plans for the fort while heading in the direction of the city."

"Ah, but he has a pass signed by General Arnold himself. I cannot fly in the face of General Arnold. He would have my head. What are you suggesting I do?"

"Sir, I have had recent communication from our network in the city that there may a plot afoot to capture General Washington himself. I even believe that General Arnold may be a party to this plot."

"Upon my word, man! You can't be serious!"

"I am quite serious, Colonel, and I believe we must act accordingly."

The colonel clasped his hands behind his back and turned to walk across the room and back again. "This is too absurd to believe, Major. If you are wrong, it will be the devil to pay for your mistake."

"I will take full responsibility if I am wrong, Colonel." Once again Colonel Jameson walked to the other side of the room and then back again.

"Oh, very well, Tallmadge. Send a rider after the prisoner and have him returned here."

The major stepped out, and Colonel Jameson sat down at his desk. He pulled out pen and ink.

"I will have to send a note to General Arnold about this. I am not sure what he has in mind, but I don't want to risk his wrath."

Little did Jameson realize that his note would spare General Arnold from the same fate that now awaited Andre. General Arnold would flee to New York City and begin a new life on the other side of the conflict. He became despised in America as a traitor. In England he achieved neither wealth nor respect and died in relative poverty.

25
The Plot Thickens

Earle sat as his desk smoking his pipe. He wore a sour expression as he looked over at his brother who was lying on the couch snoozing.

"Wake up and listen to me, John." There was no response from the couch so Earle walked over and shook his brother. "Wake up, John, and listen to me. We need to take action if we don't want to lose this."

"Hunh, what the, oh," John Henry sounded groggy as he tried to clear his head. "Lose what, Earle? We don't even know what they have."

"We know that Adam thought there was something valuable in the trunk. I didn't know Adam very well, but he wasn't prone to exaggeration."

"What could possibly be in the trunk that was all that valuable? Maybe it was just some old clothes."

"No, he told me there was a legal paper in it that looked like a deed of some sort. He couldn't remember the location, but any piece of land is valuable these days. Do you know how much land on Long Island is worth today? It's a pretty penny, I can tell you that. Of course, it may not be in the trunk at all. That old crow may have found it and hidden it at her home. She is probably just teasing us with that trunk to make us think that's where it is. She has the deed hidden away somewhere."

"Why don't we just wait till she dies, and then we can move in. We are her nearest relatives, you know."

"Yes, we are relatives, but you know how she is. She could give away her money to charity or that church of hers. She might even give her money to that girl who takes care of her."

"Maybe we should try being nice to her."

Earle gave his brother a cold stare. "I am being nice to her. I have been calling her and asking how she is. Do you know what she said? She wanted to know if I want to come over and mow her lawn. Can you picture me mowing her lawn?"

"What about getting a lawn service?"

"Not on your life. Do you know how much those cost? She should have that girl do it."

"I thought you just called and asked her about the trunk."

"I did that, and she just snapped at me. She is lucky she has a relative who gives her a call once in a while."

"So what do we do now, Earle? We really need her money. When Uncle Oliver died he left us a half million but that didn't last as long as we thought it would. Now my credit cards are maxed out. At this rate I may have to try and get a job."

Once again Earle stared at his brother. "Maybe that wouldn't be such a bad idea." Now it was John Henry's turn to stare. Earle broke the ice. "Listen to me, little brother. Call it a hunch if you want, but I believe that trunk holds the key to our dilemma.

Nevertheless, we should pursue our original goal. Since Sadie doesn't respond to our friendly overtures, we have to gain her resources the hard way. We have to have her declared mentally unstable or at least collect evidence of it. That way if she passes away and leaves her fortune to charity we can challenge the will."

"That shouldn't be difficult to prove. She does odd things all the time.

*   *   *

My fingers extended toward the ground bouncing the ball three times as was my custom. Lifting the racket up I peered over the rackethead at my grandfather who was waiting at the far end of the court. This was it. All the bragging rights were riding on this next point. I tossed the ball into the air just higher than my racket could reach. My legs crouched and then I sprang up and smacked the ball with a sharp upper cut imparting topspin. The ball landed just inside the service box and Gramps reached for it. His return was coming back fast until it hit the top of the tape and dropped on his side of the net.

"Well, that's game, set, and match kiddo. We had better stop since my ego can't take much more of a beating."

"Hey, it was 7-5, 7-5 so I wouldn't call that a beating. Besides, you won the last two times we played, so it really was my turn to win."

"Yes, but you keep getting tougher, and I keep running out of gas."

"You may have to cut down on those cheeseburgers and hot fudge sundaes."

"I don't think *you* ever met a dish of ice cream you couldn't eat."

"I am just trying to help you improve your tennis game, Gramps."

We both grabbed towels and water bottles and headed to the lawn chairs near the court to cool off.

"What have you heard from your parents, Greta?"

"They are in Saint Andrews. Dad said he wanted to see the golf museum there."

"It sounds like they are having a great trip."

"They said they miss us a lot, but I don't see how they have much time to miss us. Well, they are coming back next week. When does Gram come back?"

"We need to pick her up from the airport tomorrow. She will have a lot to tell us and plenty of pictures, I am sure. Rick and Becky now have three lovely girls with the addition of little Rose."

"I can hardly wait to go see them in person."

"Pictures will have to do until your folks get back."

"What are we going to do now, Gramps?"

"Do you mean about dinner, or do you mean about the trunk?"

"I was thinking about the trunk, but since you mentioned dinner, that's a good question, too."

"Dinner is an easy fix. I have a coupon for Salvatori's Pizza in my pocket. The trunk is a tougher problem."

"Why don't we go to Salvatori's and discuss the trunk there?"

"I like how you think, kiddo. It's right down the street."

We got in Gramps's Jeep and turned in the direction of Salvatori's. In many ways it was the local teen hangout, but Gramps enjoyed going there as well as I did. A few minutes later we pulled into the parking lot and parked as far away as possible. It was one of Gramps's idiosyncrasies that he wanted to get more exercise by parking far away. I didn't question him about it anymore. I just figured he was one of a kind.

Once inside, Gramps stepped up to the counter and ordered our favorite sausage and black olive pizza with extra cheese. We had eaten out enough these past two weeks to know what we each liked. I took two plastic glasses and filled his with Dr. Pepper and mine with ginger ale while he paid for the meal. Sometimes we met some of my friends here and sometimes we would see someone he knew. This night I wanted Gramps to myself so we could talk.

The pizza arrived and we began to make short work of it when the front door opened.

"Oh no. Not him," I said and put my hands over my face and began to slowly sink beneath the table. Gramps turned to look and saw a teenage boy with a Red Sox cap perched backwards on his head. The boy was looking around until he spotted Gramps and came trotting over.

"Hi, Mr. Webb. I was hoping you and Greta would be here. Hi, Greta." I quit slipping under the table and pulled myself up while the boy sat down with us.

"Jeremy, what are you doing here?" I asked with an unwelcoming attitude.

"I came looking for you and your grandfather, of course. I saw you two at the courts and figured you might be heading this way. Hey, sausage and black olive – my favorite."

"Help yourself, young man. You can help us finish it."

"I don't think we needed any help, but go ahead, Jeremy. You must be getting ready for the summer tournament."

"I sure am. Last year I went three rounds and this year I'm gonna do even better." He was stuffing the pizza in his mouth while talking, making it a little difficult to understand him.

"I haven't seen you at the courts recently, Greta. I thought with your folks gone you would be here every day. What have you been up to?"

"We have been doing some research, young man. There really is more to life than tennis."

"Of course there is, Mr. Webb, but not when the weather is this good. What have you been researching?"

Gramps decided to defer to me to answer this and looked my way. I let out a sigh, and then resigning myself to the fact that Jeremy had imposed on our table, decided to answer him.

"We have been studying the Revolutionary War and General Washington's spy ring. You probably wouldn't be interested in it."

Jeremy grabbed the last slice of pizza and said, "Oh cool! I sure would. Remember, my last name is Butler. My family came over from England. I know a lot about the Revolutionary War. What do you want to know? Just ask me. Go ahead."

"Okay then, who was a spy living in New York who gave Washington a heads-up on counterfeit colonial dollars being printed?"

Jeremy paused more to think than to chew his pizza, which was what he should have been focused on. "You got me on that one, but I always say that more important than names and dates is the 'why' the war happened in the first place."

"Okay, smarty pants, why *did* the war happen in the first place?" I challenged him.

"Well, a lot of people would give you a trite answer like 'No taxation without representation,' but that's just an overused phrase that stands for the real reason for the war."

"Okay then, tell us the real reason for the war, Jeremy Butler." I hoped that I wasn't turning red or something.

"Are you ready?" he asked us.

We both looked at him now, giving him the freedom to share his profound insight.

"'Control' is the key word here. The British wanted to control the colonies – not to mention the rest of the British Empire. They were power mad and they wanted to control everything."

Gramps tried to be accepting of Jeremy's opinion. "That's an interesting insight you have there, Jeremy."

"Well, I think that's what causes all the problems in today's world," Jeremy added. "Everybody tries to control everybody else. That's what causes wars. That's what causes terrorism and divorce and murder and crime and all the bad things that take place in the world. If people just left other people alone, then everything would be great. Hey, can we order another pizza?"

After thirty minutes and a second large pizza, we finally said goodbye to Jeremy and got in the Jeep. As we drove home, I couldn't help thinking about our conversation and Jeremy ruining our dinner.

"We were having a fun time till Jeremy showed up. He is so opinionated. I suppose some of what he said is true. When people try to control other people, they make a lot of problems. What do you think, Gramps? Should everybody just leave each other alone?"

"Well, kiddo, there is some truth in what Jeremy had to say. England did want to get back something for what they considered investing in the colonies. You could also say that the colonists believed England was trying to control them in order to do it. No representation sure sounds like control without really giving the colonists a fair hearing."

"So control is always a bad thing?"

"I wouldn't say that, Greta. I better be in control of this Jeep or we might crash. If parents don't maintain control over a toddler, he might wander out into the street. As a child grows, a wise parent will begin to relinquish control as a young person demonstrates wisdom in making decisions. When it comes to relationships with people, we could make a mistake by trying to control them. However, an integral part of a relationship is being an influence on one another. When we talk to each other and do things together, we influence one another. We need to try to influence people in a good way. I hope I am a good influence on you, Greta. Just between you and me, I think you are a good influence on me."

"How so, Gramps? How could I possibly be a good influence on you?"

"In many ways, Greta." He paused and then added, "I am a better driver when I think you might follow my example some day in the way you drive. I also like to see you smile and laugh when something funny happens. You are a real encouragement to me, Greta." We looked at each other and shared a warm smile.

"We still have a big problem, Gramps."

"What's that, kiddo?"

"We don't know what to do with that trunk."

26

The Trail to Yorktown

March 1781 – The Trail to Yorktown

"Robert, may I have a word with you?"

"Certainly, Mr. Rivington. What can I do for you?"

"Step into my office for a moment. This is something that must be kept quiet." The two men moved to a door that led to an office in the back of the coffeehouse.

"We have been working together for these months, Robert, and I believe it is time we were completely honest with one another."

"What do you mean, Mr. Rivington? I have always been truthful with you," Robert replied while wiping his hands nervously.

"Yes, I believe you, Robert. You have always told me the truth but not always the whole truth, I think." Robert started to protest, and Rivington held up a hand to stop him.

"You do not work here for the financial advantages, Robert. The business is not profitable enough to warrant that. I don't think you work here for a love of the clientele with the possible exception of Miss Sarah." Now both men fixed their eyes on each other with the mention of Sarah, but once again Rivington held a hand up so he could continue uninterrupted. "I believe you are here because of your cause. To be specific, your Patriot cause."

Robert looked shocked and just stared at him for a moment as the words sunk in. Then he broke the silence.

"Mr. Rivington, I will neither deny nor affirm what you are accusing me of. I believe I know you well enough by now to know that you are not a Loyalist despite what most people think of you."

"No, Robert, you are right in that. I am not a Loyalist. I freely own that to you because I believe that undoubtedly you are a Patriot Whig. I also believe you are more than just a Patriot." He paused and lowered his voice. "You are a spy for Washington!"

Townsend's mouth dropped open and he took a step back while holding up both hands as if to stop the proprietor from speaking. After a moment he said, "If you truly believe that, then why haven't you called the Redcoats to come clap me in irons or even worse?"

"It's very simple, my boy." He now paused as if he desired to create a dramatic effect. "I want you to get a message through to General Washington."

Robert took another step back at this announcement. Then he slowly raised his right hand and waved the index finger at the coffeehouse proprietor and newspaper editor. "You are playing me the fool, sir. This is one of your senseless jests."

"Not at all, my dear boy. I am in earnest. I have come upon some vital information and I wish to give it to the general. Let me state that another way. I wish to *sell* it to General Washington. Although I am sensitive to the Patriot cause, I do have to make a living."

"And you think I can arrange for the *sale* to take place?"

"Not at all, Robert. I *know* you can arrange for the sale to take place. Do you take me for a simpleton, Robert? I know you have been here just to collect information. You couldn't do it in your shop where customers go to conduct business, so you came to work here where customers like to talk. Customers here include many British officers and Tories who have no business in your shop. Come now, Robert. I will guard your secret. I just want to make contact because I have something of value to your cause."

"I will play your little game, Mr. Rivington. What do you have that you want to sell?"

"As you well know, Robert, in addition to this coffeehouse, I run a printing business. The Crown has given me the task of printing a set of signals used between British ships to communicate orders. A copy of that page should be worth perhaps as much as, let's say, five hundred pounds in British Sterling."

"Five hundred pounds? For one piece of paper? Surely you jest!"

"Not at all, my lad. Can you picture a naval battle? The British fleet will be communicating to each other while the French and Patriot fleet admirals know their every move. Five hundred pounds would be a paltry sum for a piece of paper like that."

"Yes, but how can Washington know that your paper is true? How can he trust you?"

"I have thought of that already. He *can't* trust me, so I have the solution." Once again Rivington paused for his words to sink in. "*I* will trust *him*. He must send an emissary to collect the paper. The emissary must give me Washington's word that I will receive the five hundred pounds when the paper is used and has been proved accurate. What do you say, Robert? Do we have an agreement?"

"Let me just say that *I* will keep *your* secret. I will not cause you danger by revealing what you have shared with me to the *wrong* people." At this statement the men paused and their eyes met. Robert then stretched out his hand to meet Rivington's, and they knew they had an agreement.

*   *   *

Toward the close of June 1781, Washington's headquarters occupied Pierre Van Cortlandt's Upper Manor House in New York. Pierre and his wife, Joanna, were very kind to offer this home to me, thought Washington. The general did his best to show appreciation to those who hosted him. They were at risk if the enemy ever advanced to this area.

General Washington was hovering over his map table as he studied the surrounding territories. He had a decision to make. At least he hoped it was *his* decision to make. The alliance with the French at times seemed to be one of strange bedfellows. Lafayette was one of his most trusted aides and gave him encouragement as well as true friendship. He had made it clear from the beginning that he was there to serve Washington and to learn from him. There were others the general could trust to follow his instructions as well. The French high command was not of the same mind, though. Perhaps every commander had the desire to make the key tactical decisions of how to outwit the enemy. Nevertheless, having the French as allies must be considered an opportunity. He had to take advantage of their troops as well as the naval power that could be brought to bear on the British forces.

There were two tempting targets on the map. General Cornwallis had taken his troops to the Yorktown, Virginia, area. They were separated from the forces of Sir Henry Clinton in New York City. Washington felt he could attack one of the two and win a major victory. It must be done soon, however. The French were available now for a limited time. He had no authority over them. They could pick up and leave at any moment. Washington had met with the French general Rochambeau earlier that day. Washington wanted to take the city of New York. He felt it was ripe for plucking. He had been pushed out of the city a few years before and he yearned to return. The inhabitants at one time leaned more toward supporting the Crown, but they had been treated poorly by the British and their loyalties had suffered on that account.

Rochambeau, on the other hand, desired to attack Cornwallis in Virginia. It was a smaller force and thus more vulnerable. To conquer either target, Washington knew, would require naval support. There was a French fleet moored in the West Indies led by Admiral *Comte de Grasse*. Washington had prepared a message to send to de Grasse asking for him to sail to New York and engage the British as soon as possible. Little did Washington know that Rochambeau had also prepared a message for de Grasse. His message requested the admiral to sail to Chesapeake Bay and bottle up Cornwallis cutting off his retreat. Yes, the French were his allies, but they had their own ideas. A frigate was dispatched to carry the competing messages to the *Comte de Grasse.*

In mid-August, Admiral de Grasse received the notes while in Haiti. He replied to Rochambeau that he would sail to Chesapeake Bay with twenty-eight ships of the line. He avoided normal shipping lanes on this trip and was able to surprise two

British frigates upon his arrival. They were trapped and could not get word back to the British high command.

A fleet of nineteen British ships of the line commanded by Sir Thomas Graves had already set sail toward Chesapeake Bay. The two fleets became aware of each other and began to position themselves for battle. Neither knew the full strength of the opposition. Washington and Rochambeau had by then crossed the Hudson River and were heading to Yorktown.

September 5, 1781 – Battle of Chesapeake Bay

Sir Henry Clinton kept an eye on Washington's troop movements in New York. General Clinton had been fooled into thinking Washington might attack New York because some colonial troops had been left in White Plains. Clinton sent Admiral Graves to intercept the French fleet, which they believed was heading in the direction of the Chesapeake Bay in Virginia. The French under Admiral de Grasse had arrived first and taken control of Chesapeake Bay. De Grasse was expecting the arrival of French Admiral de Barras coming from Rhode Island. At about 9:00 a.m. on the morning of September 5, sails were spotted on the horizon. In the distance the French thought the oncoming ships belonged to de Barras. The French were moving supplies ashore when the British began to approach. If the British had attacked immediately, they would have had an advantage, but they did not act. When the French realized the newly arriving ships were British, they cut their anchors off in order to get their ships underway quickly and meet the threat.

The opposing fleets began to maneuver their positions to prepare for battle. Neither fleet could accurately assess the strength of the other. The changing winds made maneuvering a challenge for both fleets. The French fleet at times seemed to anticipate the movements of the British ships. It seemed as if they could read the British naval signals between ships. At about 4:15 in the afternoon, firing began to commence in earnest. For the next two hours, the battle raged with the British suffering the most. Because of the winds and tide, the British had their lower decks below water at times and were unable to fire cannon. Six ships were badly damaged with ninety men killed and 246 wounded. The French had only two ships with severe damage and 209 casualties.

At sunset the fighting broke off so the fleets could assess the damage. Graves was reluctant to reengage in the fight as he noticed that Admiral de Barras had arrived to reinforce the French fleet. The *Comte de Grasse* now had thirty-six ships of the line at his disposal. The British only had nineteen with similar firepower. The French slipped back into the bay and the British withdrew, knowing they could not dislodge the French fleet. Cornwallis was now cut off from being supplied or evacuated by sea. He was on his own.

*   *   *

Washington and Rochambeau moved their forces and began a siege of Cornwallis at Yorktown on September 28, 1781. A combined force of 8,800 colonists and 7,800 French faced a British and German force of about 6,000. On October 9, Washington began to press his advantage by bombarding the British positions. Then on October 14, a two-pronged attack was made against the British defenses, called redoubts. Alexander Hamilton led the attack on Redoubt no. 10. The colonial force captured ground and set up artillery to fire on the town and ships in the harbor. General Washington lit the fuse for the first cannon shot from this position. The closer artillery fire now wreaked havoc on the British and German troops.

The culmination of the battle seemed inevitable when on October 17, a British officer rode toward the colonial forces while waving a white flag. Cornwallis faced the reality that his position was indefensible. The bombardment now ceased, and surrender negotiations began. The surrender took place on October 19, and General Cornwallis refused to attend. He claimed he was ill and sent his second-in-command. British general Charles O'Hara first offered his sword to Rochambeau, who gestured to Washington to receive it. General Washington in turn refused the sword and directed it be given to his second-in-command. Benjamin Lincoln received the sword and perhaps seven thousand British and Hessian troops were taken prisoner.

The news of the British defeats in the Chesapeake Bay and then Yorktown traveled to London quickly. Lord North, the British prime minister, remarked, "It's all over," when told of the defeat. Washington moved his troops to New Windsor, New York, and remained there until the war formally ended with the Treaty of Paris on September 3, 1783.

27
The Homecoming

There are many things that I appreciate about Gramps and Gram. I think that what I like most is the way they still keep the romance going. I know of couples who after years of marriage seem to lose patience with one another. Gramps told me once that even though they were getting older, he and Gram both wanted to keep trying in their relationship. They wanted to be patient to a fault. They wanted to be considerate. There were times when it wasn't easy, but it was worth the effort. It gave me a sense of security that my parents were making the effort and so were Gramps and Gram.

Gramps and I were standing at the gate waiting for passengers to disembark. Gramps held a bouquet of flowers. Two men stood nearby and couldn't help but glance at the flowers. "So who are the flowers for?" one of them asked.

"My wife, of course." Then Gramps added, "We have only been married for forty-two years."

"Nice, how do you do it?"

"Well, God gets the glory, my wife gets the credit, and I get the benefits."

Both men looked wide-eyed at this answer. Just then their wives walked up and gave them hugs.

"I brought you flowers but this man stole them from me so I am empty-handed," one of the men said. His wife winked and smiled at Gramps. "Yes, I am sure that's what happened."

A silver-haired lady now stepped up and hugged both Gramps and me at the same time. "What a great welcoming committee."

"We tried to get a brass band, but they were all booked this afternoon."

"That's just fine, sweetheart. You two are much better than any old band."

"We can't wait to tell you what we have been discovering, Gram," I said.

"I had a feeling you two were up to something. You can fill me in as we get the luggage, but first you have to hear about little Rose. As you already know, she is healthy with a pair of lungs on her that leaves no doubt about her disposition. Mom is doing well, and somehow Dad survived the ordeal. I can't wait to get home and show you my pictures."

I did most of the talking while we were waiting for the luggage to come through the carousel. Gramps filled in a few details that he thought would be helpful. We reviewed the events starting with the auction and ending with our latest visit with Aunt Sadie.

"You would enjoy meeting Aunt Sadie, Gram. She is a real sweetheart," I told her.

"Once you get past the outer crust," added Gramps.

"It also sounds like you two have been studying a lot of history."

"That's right, Gram. I have always been interested in history, but I never knew it could be this exciting. Events seem more real when you go visit the places where history actually happened."

"These two nephews seem to be a real concern, though. Did you call the police?" Gram turned to her husband of forty-two years.

"We went by the police station and filled out a report. I told them my suspicion but had to admit that I wasn't sure about identifying them. We hid the contents of the box away as well as the box itself. If they broke in again, I am sure they could never find it."

"That isn't exactly comforting, Joshua."

"Well, Julie, I still don't understand why those two are willing to break the law for that trunk. As interesting as it is, the monetary value is no more than a week's pay for a typical worker."

"Come now, Joshua. Since when do thieves think about how they could make money being honest? We just need to make sure the house is protected and ourselves as well. Did Greta's parents get home yet?"

I spoke up as Gramps grabbed Gram's luggage. "They are due in on Friday, Gram. You will just have to put up with me for a couple more days."

"You know I don't think that way, my dear. You liven our humble place up considerably. Just don't buy any more mystery boxes. At least not until you figure out what to do with this one."

I seemed to talk nonstop now, as the three of us drove back to the house.

"So you took a trip to Long Island, did you?"

"Yes, the visit with the Kims was marvelous. Professor Kim is a fountain of knowledge and filled us in on some Revolutionary War facts. Then we visited Oyster Bay and Setauket. I will have to take you to see Raynham Hall someday, if you can stay home long enough for me to plan it."

"Now, Joshua, you want me to go help with newborns almost as much as I want to go, so don't complain."

"Yes, you represent us, and I know our kids appreciate your help tending to the house while they get adjusted to the new addition."

"We don't have any more babies scheduled that I know of. Maybe I will help you with your mystery box."

"That would be fine with me. If I could just determine why some people think it is valuable enough to want to steal it, then I would sleep better. The two nephews don't appear to be collectors or history buffs."

"You never had any trouble sleeping for any reason, Joshua, but maybe there is something that doesn't meet the eye just yet. Tell me more about this mystery box of yours." It was a forty-five minute drive home, and the two of us filled in many details.

"So you see, Julie, what we found in the box really was fascinating."

"Granted, but not what people would want to steal," responded Gram.

"I can only believe that the nephews have been deluding themselves about the contents."

"Have you called the nephews to let them know what is in the box?"

"I thought about that, but I feel awkward talking to someone I think burglarized our home. Can you picture what I might say? 'Listen fellas, this is what was in the box so you don't have to break in and try to steal it again. Why don't you come over for a glass of lemonade and look at the contents?'"

"That sounds pretty good to me. You usually try the honest straightforward approach, Joshua, and it often works."

"Maybe I will, Julie, but I want to think about it for a while. Right now I just want to enjoy you being home again."

We pulled into the driveway and paused while I got out and checked the mail. "Haven't you been communicating with your parents through email, Greta?"

"Yes, Gram, but they have been sending postcards as well. It's a lot of fun to get cards from another country. Here's one now."

"Great, what does it say?"

"The card is a picture of Stirling Castle in Scotland. I have been studying about the United Kingdom for the past several months. I figured it would help me feel more a part of their trip. This card says there were two tour guides and both were named Michael. Isn't that a kick?"

"That's not too surprising, dear. Michael is a very popular name in Scotland."

"Here's another card with a picture on it of British soldiers wearing their famous red uniforms."

"Yes, of course. That's why they were called Redcoats. That's also why they were good targets for the colonists to shoot at. It makes you wonder who thought that one through. Can you picture it? The British were wearing red and marched on the road while Americans had on brown or buckskin and hid behind trees."

"I get it. That must be why our army today wears camouflage," I said. Just then Skipper ran out the door and greeted one and all with unbridled enthusiasm.

"Ah, Skipper, it is good to see you too," said Gram as she stroked the little dog's back. "Have they been feeding you regularly?"

"Greta wouldn't let Skipper starve. You know that," said Gramps.

"Now where is this mystery box you two have been talking about? I want to share in the excitement."

"It's down in the basement covered with some blankets."

"I might as well take a look at it before I make dinner."

The three of us made our way down the basement stairs and uncovered our mystery box. Gram looked at the trunk, and her face showed a deep interest in the old antique.

"We stacked the contents over on this shelf," said Gramps. He pointed to the items that were visible, and Gram picked up the copy of *Common Sense*. She thumbed through the book very carefully.

"I have never actually read this book, but I have heard about it for many years. It was very instrumental in shaping the feelings of Americans during the Revolutionary War. If this is one of the early copies, then that is an amazing find indeed."

"Have you heard of James Rivington's *Royal Gazette*, Julie? It was a newspaper published during the war in New York City, and it gives insight into how the citizens were feeling at that time. Here are some copies of that newspaper."

Gram took the papers from Gramps and intently pored over them. Then I handed the letters to her.

"Here are the most amazing items of all, Gram. These are letters that were written during the war between sweethearts living in New York." Gram took the letters as well.

"I can see why you two have been so involved in this. You go to an auction and buy an old trunk, and it turns back the pages of history for you. Let me see the inside of the trunk."

Gramps leaned over and opened the lid. It still smelled very musty. "Have you got a flashlight so I can get a closer look at it?" asked Gram.

Gramps walked over to his workbench and fished around in a drawer and came back with a flashlight. He shined it inside for better illumination of the trunk. Gram studied the interior for a moment, then took the flashlight from him and held it closer.

"There is something a little peculiar about this, Joshua."

"What do you mean, Julie?"

"Look at the bottom. It may be my imagination, but it doesn't look level to me. Is the floor level?"

Once again Gramps went to his workbench and came back this time with a level. First, he placed it on the floor to confirm that the floor was level, and then he placed it inside the trunk and saw that the bottom had a definite tilt.

"Well, how do you like that? Not only is the bottom not level, but it looks like the inside bottom is about four or five inches higher than the outside bottom. Ladies, it looks like our mystery trunk holds another mystery. It has a false bottom."

28
Tying Up Loose Ends

It was common knowledge that negotiations were taking place to bring the war to an end. The surrender of Cornwallis had brought the curtain down on this fierce conflict between two now distinct nations. There were winners and losers in this struggle. People now had to make decisions about what course to take without the shedding of blood. The victors and the vanquished must now move on to play a new role on the world's stage.

*   *   *

Sarah and her father stood on the deck and watched the sailors busily hoist sails and tie ropes to enable the ship to cast off. The gentleman looked down at his daughter with concern. She had a look about her that could tell no lies. Her heart had become knit together with someone she now had to leave behind.

"My dear, you need not be so cast down. We are beginning a new adventure. Nova Scotia is said to be a land of the proverbial milk and honey. We will find a place there. It is sad to leave your sister here, but she now has her own husband to look after. I am thankful that I still have you to look after me. Without Mother and your sisters, you are all I have to depend on. Would that events had been resolved in a different fashion."

"Oh Father, I am grateful to be able to be with you. I am sad to leave Margaret and others whom I consider to be my friends. We may never see them again. Margaret will travel to London with her husband. They should fare very well. It saddens me to leave some I know here in New York." Her voice trailed off as she thought of the one person she felt a deep pain over leaving. She could not even trust herself to see him face to face. She had sent him a letter. What a coward she was, but she could not even trust her feelings.

"Yes, this is a strange and somewhat barbaric land. They have achieved independence. The question now is, will they be able to govern themselves? There are wise men here. There are also those who only seek their own gain. I suppose that is the case wherever we might travel. I believe opportunities for me lie to the north. We will do very well there."

"I have no doubt of your success, Father. You always find ways to improve our situation. I am curious about the future of this land. No king will rule them. They have a Congress that has difficulty making decisions. France may now invade and claim the colonies for themselves. Spain is like a vulture that could fly down and take what it wants. Without the stability of the British Empire, these colonies may go back to the Indians."

"Nonsense, my daughter. As I said, there are good men here. Even though I have spoken ill of Washington on many occasions, he has proved himself to be a strong and even a wise leader. If he can conquer the finest army in the world, he will be able to lead the colonies in peace. I even heard they may make him their king. What do you think of that, my dear?"

"Oh Father, I do not think that will happen. They have fought these many years to throw off a king. Do you really think they would crown one now?"

"Perhaps not, but there are some able men here who could lead the colonists. There are men like Franklin and Jefferson. It is said that Washington will continue to trust Providence to lead this land. You need not be concerned about the future of America."

Sarah was deep in thought about what she was leaving behind more than where she was going. She was leaving a friend whom she had worked with and shared secrets as well as dangers. She felt she had to leave now as the last unmarried daughter. Her father needed her. She could not abandon him. But what of Robert?

*   *   *

Benjamin Tallmadge rode with three other officers down the long road leading to the city. Gawkers stood along the road and stared at them. Some soldiers wearing the red British uniform fell in with them. Others carrying weapons but not in uniform joined the procession. They had stopped at several sentry checkpoints along the way. The white flag of truce they carried to this point was being honored. Colonel Tallmadge had requested permission from Washington to make this trip. He knew the city was in transition from war to peace, and he was concerned.

Everyone knew that a peace treaty was being negotiated in Paris, and the British would be leaving soon. Tory Loyalists were feeling very uneasy. Some were living in homes that had belonged to Patriots, and they knew they would have to give them up. Other Loyalists were living in homes they had legitimately purchased, but they were afraid they would be evicted. Their support of the Crown was common knowledge, and Patriots resented them. Many had left to return to England or to start a new life in Canada.

Tallmadge was riding into town to address a special concern. He had contacts in the city who were falsely considered to be Loyalists. They were his spies. They had worked in the city and associated with military personnel in order to gain information. Now their work was finished, but no one knew that they were Patriots instead of Loyalists. Colonel Tallmadge was on a mission to secure the safety of these spies. If necessary, he would hire bodyguards to protect them.

*   *   *

Colonel Tallmadge was more than a little surprised when General Guy Carleton invited him to dine with the British command officers. Carleton had replaced Clinton as British military commander in New York. As Tallmadge entered the dining room, he recognized one of the Redcoats standing guard at the door. He nodded slightly toward the man in recognition but quickly entered the officers' area.

Carleton greeted him warmly, "It is a pleasure to dine with you, Colonel Tallmadge. I must own that I wish the circumstances were not as they are. Nevertheless, we must come to grips with reality."

"Yes, General Carleton, I believe we share the relief that hostilities are at an end. The negotiations in Paris will be to simply iron out final details. I will be glad to send your regards to General Washington when I see him."

"I do not wish to spoil our evening, but I must mention my disappointment at the demise of poor Major Andre. We had always felt that he was destined for greater things had he been given the opportunity. I understood your need to make an example. I just wish we could have arranged a prisoner exchange."

"If you recall, sir, General Washington was willing to make an exchange, but your leadership at the time was not."

"Ah yes, I recall you wanted General Arnold to be exchanged for Andre. I was sympathetic to that proposal, but surely you realize that an exchange for Arnold would have been quite impossible. It seems that General Arnold has been a problem to both sides in this war."

"How so, General Carleton?"

"My introduction to General Arnold came at Valcour Island. He tricked us into a most disadvantageous position on the water. Then he maneuvered past us and led a merry chase to Fort Ticonderoga. I can laugh about it now, but at the time I was furious." Tallmadge couldn't help but smile at the thought of Carleton's frustration.

"Then, a year later, we credited his courage at Saratoga for causing Burgoyne to surrender. While Gates stayed in his tent, Arnold took the field and inspired your side to victory. Yes, Arnold's courage cannot be questioned."

"That's right, General Carleton. At the time he was an honored and loyal Patriot general," Tallmadge agreed. "It wasn't till later that his true colors were shown. We could debate which virtue is greater – courage or loyalty. Arnold has courage, but he fell far short on loyalty."

Carleton leaned toward his dinner guest and in a low voice said, "Yes, Colonel. We are actually in agreement on that. Nevertheless we could not give him up."

"I understand that now and understood it then, but that is what led to the conclusion of the matter as it happened. It cannot now be modified, so let us speak of more pleasant subjects."

"Quite so, Colonel Tallmadge. Let us drink a toast." Everyone raised their glasses with the two men.

"To a lasting peace," spoke the general.

The officers echoed, "To a lasting peace."

*   *   *

Nov 25, 1783

General Washington rode down the New York street to the cheers of citizens. The officers with him rode eight abreast. Washington knew full well that most of the crowd who cheered had been just as jubilant for the British officers and army only a day earlier. Such were the fortunes of war. As they turned a corner, they came to a bookshop and the general dismounted. Turning to Hamilton, he said, "This gentleman has some books that I would like to purchase." The officers in the procession tried to mask their astonishment. The name "James Rivington" was stenciled on the window. He was well known to be a Tory and a scoundrel.

Once inside, Washington was approached by the proprietor himself, who was wearing an ink-stained apron.

"Your Excellency. You are honoring my humble shop. How may I serve you?"

"It seems my interests are soon to be returning to my farm at Mount Vernon. I was wondering if you have any good books dealing with the subject of agriculture."

"Step into my office, if you please, sir. I may not have the right book in stock, but I can certainly order one for you." The two men stepped into the private office of the proprietor. Both Tallmadge and Hamilton waited outside the office door and tried not to listen to the muffled words that were spoken. Tallmadge thought he could hear some coins jingle behind the door. A moment later, the two men stepped back into the main room.

"Yes, Mr. Rivington, I would appreciate it if you would have those books sent to Mount Vernon when they arrive."

"I certainly will, sir. It may take a few months for them to arrive, but you have made a very good choice. I want to wish you well in your new interest, sir. I am confident in your continued success in whatever you do." The two shook hands, and Washington stepped out the door followed by his two officers. Once outside, all the men mounted and continued on their tour.

Later that evening, General Washington dined with his officers. It was not a boisterous time of celebration. The war was indeed at an end, but the men felt that their lives were now going in separate directions. They had been through so much together. They had faced dangers. They had plotted the course that brought first survival and then ultimately victory to their side. Now they knew they must return to a life of peace. The war had lasted eight long years.

The commander-in-chief rose to his feet and looked about him at the men who had been at his side during the trying times of war.

"Gentlemen, my heart is very divided. We have so much to celebrate. The fortunes of war have been directed by Providence to give us victory over a great and, I must say, noble foe. We look around this room and know there are faces missing that we will never see again. We have toasted victory, and now we will go our separate ways. We cannot know the future, but we can look to the past without regret. I have no more commands to give you in the line of duty. I only have this request. Will each of you give me your hand before we part ways?"

The men rose to their feet and one by one bid farewell to their undisputed leader. The war was over, and these men must now begin life fresh in a new nation. The burdens they had borne together would not soon be forgotten. The future was full of promise and hope. Victory had never tasted so good.

29

The Secret in the Box

Not being able to see gave me an overwhelming sense of unbelief. I knew my eyes were open, but I had no way of proving it. That's how dark it was. In my heart I knew I was perfectly safe. Gramps and Gram were in their bed down the hall, and Skipper was snoring through some pleasant dreams at the foot of my bed. I just couldn't sleep. My thoughts kept going over the day that was now complete. That box had done it again. It had given us one more surprise.

One of the simple pleasures in life is surprising someone. I had a blast the time I got up early on a Saturday and made Mom and Dad breakfast in bed. They refused to stay in bed to eat it, though. At first I was a little miffed that they wouldn't stay in bed. Then again, who really wants to eat while lying down. I think Gramps enjoyed surprising Gram on a regular basis. He did it again today. As I lay wide awake I thought about the day's events.

Gram had opened the door leading into the basement and called down. "Dinner is ready, Joshua. You and Greta need to quit playing around with that box and come up and eat something."

I smiled at Gramps and yelled, "We'll be right up, Gram. Just give us one minute."

Gram turned back to the stove and switched the burner off. She had just finished preparing some grilled cheese sandwiches. She put them on a tray and carried them to the dining room table. As she turned back, she saw my beaming face. I stepped aside and Gram opened her mouth wide in astonishment.

"What on earth are you wearing, Joshua?" Her husband stood before her sporting the brightest red coat she could ever imagine. It was shaped like a tuxedo with navy and white accent material. The length went down to Gramps's knees. Gram stared for a full minute while Gramps and I both laughed at her expression and waited for the next remark.

"That looks like a costume of a British soldier's uniform from the Revolutionary War. Where did you get it?"

Gramps continued to smile. "Actually, my dear, this is no costume. I believe it really is a British soldier's uniform from the Revolutionary War. I think it fits me pretty well," he added.

"Where did you get it? Don't tell me you found it in the box?"

"If we don't tell you we found it in the box, then we can't tell you the truth, my dear, and you wouldn't want us to lie."

"Upon my word Joshua, that is startling, but how do you know it's for real?"

"Everything else in the box has been genuine, so I have no reason to doubt that this is from the Revolutionary War period. It was in the false bottom along with another small box. It looks like we have another mystery box," he said as he brought a small wooden box from behind his back. "We need to get this box open somehow."

"Oh no," said Gram, "I am not sure I can handle any more mysteries," she mildly protested.

"Gramps! What about that key that Aunt Sadie gave you?" I reminded him.

"Yes, of course. It's worth a try. I'll go get it."

A minute later Gramps was back. Setting the new box on the table, he inserted the key. We heard a click as the lock opened. All three of us looked at one another, and then Gramps said, "Here goes nothing, folks."

He lifted the box lid and we saw folded papers inside. Gramps carefully lifted the papers out and began to unfold them. He separated the papers one by one. "This first one looks like a letter written by the same person who wrote that other letter we found, Greta. The handwriting is the same." He handed it to me.

"Wow! Slick! Take a look at this letter, Gram. Why don't you read it out loud?"

Gram took the paper from me and began to read.

March 3, 1783

My Very Dear Robert

It seems like our time together has been for a lifetime or perhaps just a few days. I cannot decide which. We have shared secrets that affected the lives of many and has resulted in drawing our hearts together as I never could have imagined.

I think back to the days when we first became acquainted. Our backgrounds were so different. We were on roads that wound in diverse directions. Then I began to change. I began to understand the world we lived in. I began to listen to you and to comprehend the events of the day. I saw that lives were changing. My home had been across the sea, but now it was in a strange new land. I had changed and it was because of you and what we had shared together.

Over the course of these months together I often pictured what the future might hold. In that future I could see happiness instead of mourning. I could see laughter and gaiety instead of long sad faces. I could see children running and giggling to meet you at the door and jump into your arms. I could see you smile as you carried them inside and put them down so we could share the time together. It gave me warmth and pleasure as nothing else could.

Do you remember our walk where we first spoke openly with one another? I knew I could trust you and you realized I would not betray you. What a perfectly charming evening it was! I so much desired that thrilling evening to go on and on. That evening was just the beginning for us. My esteem for you and my hopes for our relationship began to grow more each day. I began to believe that Providence had brought us together and Providence would keep us together for the rest of our lives.

Alas, it is not to be. We have gone through many trials together. We have shared dangers and thrills. Our common cause has brought peace to this troubled land. Yet with that peace there is still responsibility that cannot be ignored.

My dear father is taking our family to Nova Scotia. You know why we must go. My father could never be content in an independent America. You also know that as his last daughter I have an obligation to care for him in his waning years. If he were to find out the mission you and I have accomplished, it would grieve him. I cannot bear to bring him sorrow in that way.

It is for that reason that I must bid you adieu. You are the one I hold dearest, but you must know we can never be together. I will always be your affectionate

SS

Gram looked up from the yellowed page in her hands with glistening eyes.

"It sounds very sad. It's a letter between sweethearts saying goodbye. Why, I am almost crying about this. This lady is giving up her sweetheart so she will not disappoint her dear father. Why does she have to do that?"

"It's a long story, Julie, but the short version is that after the war many Loyalists felt like they had to leave since they were no longer in authority. This girl's father was a Loyalist. Since he had supported the Crown of England, some Patriots would want to punish him for it. Their property might be vandalized and looted or even taken away."

"That's terrible," exclaimed Gram. "How could people do that to them?"

"You could say it would be payback. We discovered in our research how the British mistreated colonists and confiscated property. So when the war was winding down, the Loyalists were worried. There was a lot of anarchy. It wasn't like the French Revolution where people were sent to the guillotine for next to nothing, but it wasn't very pretty either. So many Loyalists went back to England or other parts of the British Empire."

"It's still very sad," said Gram. "It sounds like this young lady had to leave the one she loved in order to be with her father."

"It also shows how a daughter can love her father enough to sacrifice her own personal happiness. That seems almost unbelievable in this day and age."

"What are the other papers about, Gramps?" I asked.

"Here is a second letter in a different handwriting. Hmm, this last paper looks more like an official document." Gramps scanned the paper he held with great interest. At last he said, "My layman's eye suggests this paper is old enough to be from the 1700s. Of course, I believe everything we have found in the box is from that century."

"One is a letter from a member of Congress to this same Robert, and the other looks like a document of some sort. It looks official and is dated February 12, 1817. It may have been an early document from the post Revolution age. Ah, that's what I was hoping for."

"What is it, Gramps? What do you see?"

"Look at the name on this document, Greta - Robert Townsend. What a find, Greta! There may have been more than one Robert Townsend during the Revolution, but then again, this trunk may have belonged to the Long Island spy who served General Washington."

Gramps handed me the document to look over. My hand trembled a bit as I tried to understand what it all meant. I could sense that this yellow piece of paper was old as could be and seemed valuable to boot.

"This looks like a description of some land." I looked up at Gramps. "Now that we have a name, what do we do?"

"I think we need to get someone else to look at this besides us. Greta, do you remember the name of Sadie's lawyer?

"I remember his name is Larsen, but we will have to call Aunt Sadie if you want to contact him."

"Yes, I will give her a call and ask if I should give him this document. He might be able to substantiate its validity."

"What's the other letter about, Gramps?"

"Well, the handwriting isn't as good as the lady's letter, and it is somewhat faded. What I can make out seems to indicate it is a thank-you and mentions the document as a sort of reward. There's also a blank page with these documents."

* * *

Two days later, Gramps's phone rang. "Joshua Webb speaking."

"Hello, Mr. Webb. This is Milton Larsen. I have been going over the documents you brought me and find them very fascinating. I will have to have them examined by others, but I also think it would be in everyone's best interests to have a meeting of the involved parties. Would you be willing to meet at Sadie's house tomorrow morning at 10:00 a.m.?"

"I would be available and am indeed interested, but it seems like only the family should be involved in this."

"That's what I thought, too, Mr. Webb, but Sadie wants you and your granddaughter there. Needless to say, what Sadie wants is what we will be doing."

"Understood, Mr. Larsen. My granddaughter and I will be happy to come and support whatever Sadie wants to do with the trunk and its contents."

He ended the call as I entered the room.

"I heard a little bit, Gramps. What do you think it's all about now? It seems like that document might be worth something after all."

"I'm still not sure about that document, Greta, but I do think a meeting would be a good idea. It will help clear the air. It may even settle some differences between Aunt Sadie and her nephews."

"So it sounds like I get to go to this meeting too?"

"From what I can tell, Aunt Sadie wouldn't have this meeting without you. I think your gingerbread cookies won her heart."

"Well, I like Aunt Sadie a lot, and I will make a fresh batch of cookies."

30
General Washington's Debt

The new nation was still in its infancy. The Treaty of Paris had officially ended the Revolutionary War, and the colonies were now faced with the daunting task of governing themselves. There would be no king. Instead there was a president and a Senate and House of Representatives. In addition each colony had its own local government. Most Americans believed that a central government was necessary to establish relations with the European countries. The first try at national government was the Articles of Confederation. All thirteen colonies had ratified it by March 1, 1781. The articles established a very weak central government, and its shortcomings led to the Constitutional Convention of 1787. The Articles of Confederation were replaced by the United States Constitution on March 4, 1789.

By 1817 there were nineteen states in the new nation. These United States had known four different presidents. George Washington had been selected unanimously by the electoral college in both his terms. Then in 1796, with Washington's retirement, elections became hotly contested. John Adams succeeded Washington as the second president when he received 71 votes to Thomas Jefferson's 68. That made Jefferson the vice president. In 1800 the electoral college tied between Jefferson and Aaron Burr and the presidency had to be determined by the House of Representatives. After thirty-six ballots Jefferson emerged the victor with Burr becoming vice president. In spite of these political tensions the transfer of power each time remained bloodless.

While Washington had the respect and admiration of the nation, politics had become a nasty business. Aaron Burr and Alexander Hamilton were in opposing political parties and the day came when their personal feud came to a head. Hamilton faced Burr in a duel on July 12, 1804, and was mortally wounded. Hamilton was a hero of the American Revolution and a leading proponent of a strong central government. Burr, who had come within one vote of being the third president, lost all political influence after that.

George Washington had supervised the building of the nation's capital on the banks of the Potomac River, but he never lived in Washington, D.C. He had served the country from locations in New York City and then in Philadelphia. There had been a second war with England that served to underscore the strength of the nation and confirm its independence.

*   *   *

The date was February 12, 1817. Benjamin Tallmadge had been serving in the House of Representatives since March 1801. James Madison, the fourth president of the United States, was due to leave office on March 4. By 1817, Tallmadge was one of the few congressmen still serving who had fought in the Revolution. He was usually a soft-spoken member of Congress. Then one day a question came to the House that got his attention. One of the men who captured John Andre had filed a petition asking for a larger pension. A day was designated for the House of Representatives to discuss the request.

The elderly gentleman walked into the chamber where his colleagues were sitting at their desks. He looked around, and it seemed all eyes were on him. He was one of the oldest members of Congress now. He sat down and refrained from making small talk with any of the others. His mind was dwelling on the business at hand. He had been considering the petition before the committee for several days now. The chairman rapped the gavel on the table and called the meeting to order. The petition was read to the group and discussion began. Several of his colleagues admitted that they were in favor of granting the petition. After all, the capture of Andre was a vital achievement that thwarted a dangerous plot.

Then one of the congressmen turned in his direction and said, "Benjamin, you were in the war we are speaking of, and I believe you are acquainted with the facts of this case. What say you to this petition?"

Benjamin Tallmadge rose to his feet to address the other committee members. It was not his habit to remind others in Congress that he had served and fought for the colonies to be able to stand on their own apart from the British Crown. This was his last session of Congress as he was soon to retire. He waited till all eyes were on him before he began to speak.

Looking around, he said, "Gentlemen, we have before us a petition to expand the pension of three men. These men are John Paulding, Isaac Van Wart, and David Williams. These are the same men who apprehended John Andre, who was an officer in the British Army. Major Andre, as we all know, was a principal agent in the defection of that scoundrel Benedict Arnold. Major Andre was not in his uniform and was behind Patriot lines at the time of his capture, so he rightly was deemed a spy and received a spy's recompense. In plain terms, he was hanged for his attention to his duties."

"The defection of Benedict Arnold and the capture of Major Andre were significant events that played out during the war. Now these three have come to call our attention to their deeds and request that their pension be expanded because of the valuable service they rendered."

"I could give you a list of thousands of men, and, yes, some women, who played valuable roles during that war. Now I must stand before you defiant and proclaim that my list does not include the names of these three. John Paulding, Isaac Van Wart, and David Williams were part of a rabble group known as Cowboys. They were on the highway that day to rob and plunder anyone who might come their way. Major Andre was unlucky enough to cross their path. When they searched him, they were not looking for evidence of espionage. They were looking for coin to steal. If Major Andre had convinced them he could pay more to be taken to the British authorities, then by God Almighty I am most assured they would have done so. Now these scoundrels have come to petition Congress to raise their pension." By this time Tallmadge's face was beet red. "I move that we reject this petition outright." With that statement he sat down.

There was now general pandemonium in the chamber. All the delegates seemed to be speaking at once. One man mentioned that if the petition was granted, there would be many more requests by others to enlarge their pensions. Three pensions could not be enlarged without enlarging all of the pensions.

Tallmadge quietly listened to the discussion. His mind was racing through a flood of memories. He had been Washington's chief of intelligence. He had taken a carriage ride with Andre during his last hours to where he was to be executed. He had been Andre's counterpart in the Continental Army. He had written down his memoirs years later, and now they raced through his mind conjured up by this disturbing request by the three highwaymen. There were many who deserved greater rewards for their service but not these three. His thoughts turned to what he believed was the most valuable service of the war he had been associated with.

The Culper spy ring had provided information to Washington that on numerous occasions had prevented disaster or facilitated success. He thought of Abraham Woodhull, who had become a judge. He thought of Caleb Brewster, who was settled down on his farm and raising a family. He thought of faithful Anna Strong who had lived in Setauket quietly after the war and passed away in 1812.

Then his thoughts turned to Robert Townsend. Townsend was still living in Oyster Bay. He remembered talking to Townsend after the war. He had suggested that Robert apply for a pension or even one of the bounty land warrants that were given to those who had fought and the widows of those who had perished. He believed that Townsend was entitled to have as much as 500 acres granted to him, yet Townsend had not applied. How odd Townsend had been. During the war, he was concerned that he would not be able to find work after the war ended. When he agreed to spy for the Patriots, he had asked Washington to give him rewards after the war, and the general had made promises. Yes, the general had made promises that he never kept. Townsend had not applied for a pension or a land grant. Maybe he kept quiet because he didn't want anyone to know about his service.

Tallmadge slammed his fist down on the table. Washington promised Townsend that he would be rewarded and he never was. Washington is gone now, but I am going to keep that promise for him, he told himself. I am going down to the war office tomorrow morning and raise Cain. What good is it to be a member of Congress if you can't get some bureaucrats to listen to you? I might even be able to do it without any publicity. Perhaps that would soothe Townsend.

His mind was now composed. He could never relax until he had a clear vision of what must be done, and now he had that vision. Tomorrow he would make sure that an old friend was not forgotten. Tallmadge had served Washington faithfully in uniform and following the war. He smiled at the thought that he would serve him after his death by keeping a promise Washington had made.

Tallmadge could sense now that the discussion was winding down. They would take a vote soon. It looked like the petition to reward these three would be voted down. His time in Congress would come to an end when this session ended. He had a sense of closure. If his plans for the morning succeeded, then he would be able to leave Congress with no unfinished business to attend to. Dear God, I pray for success, he murmured.

31
Lawyer Larsen Calls a Meeting

Gramps and I never did like meetings. The few I had been to seemed boring and often did not accomplish anything of interest. For some reason I felt that this meeting was going to be different. I couldn't imagine any get-together with Aunt Sadie would be boring.

The black Jeep Wrangler pulled into the driveway at 9:50 a.m. Gramps was a stickler for punctuality and had no intention of being late to this meeting. I had been carrying a tray of cookies on my lap for the entire ride.

"I am so excited I could bust! This seems like something out of a murder mystery. Here we are gathering all the players to go over the clues and figure out what the facts mean. It's just too bad that Hercule Poirot or Sherlock Holmes won't be there."

"I hope you aren't too disappointed, kiddo. We may just be going over some legalese on some old documents that no longer mean anything. I just hope Aunt Sadie gets some closure regarding what's in the trunk. I also hope her nephews can begin to treat her with more respect."

We got out of the Jeep and approached the front door. "It looks like we are the first ones here besides Lawyer Larsen. That red Camaro must be his car." We rang the doorbell and Marguerite welcomed us in. We followed her through the hallway to the now familiar parlor.

"Thank you, Marguerite. Good morning, Mrs. Woodruff. How are you today? Hello, Mr. Larsen."

"Now stop that 'Mrs. Woodruff' nonsense. Remember, I told you to call me Sadie. We are old friends now. How are you, dearie? My goodness did you bring cookies again? Marguerite, could you rustle us up something to drink with them? Now set yourselves down." Sadie indicated the settee. "My nephews are always late, so we will have a few minutes to chat before they get here."

Lawyer Larsen had stood up and now shook Gramps's hand.

"Mr. Webb, it's a pleasure to see you again and meet this young lady. Greta, Aunt Sadie has been saying she hoped you would bring more cookies today."

"Hello, Mr. Larsen. It's nice to meet you."

Marguerite reappeared and said, "I have some water on for tea, and it looks like your two nephews are walking up to the door, Mrs. Woodruff."

Marguerite rushed to open the door for the new arrivals. Earle and John Henry stepped into the parlor and shook hands with Lawyer Larsen and Gramps. They ignored the girls and turned to Aunt Sadie.

"You are looking great, Aunt Sadie. Have you been taking your medicine?"

"Never mind that, you two. We are not here to discuss my health. Sit yourselves down so we can get started." Sadie moved her wheelchair closer to the fireplace. There was a warm fire burning, which she seemed to appreciate.

Lawyer Larsen stood up and walked to the center of the room. "I am expecting an agent of mine to show up in a few minutes, but we might as well get started."

He cleared his throat as if he were preparing to address a jury with a closing argument in a criminal case.

"As you all know, the main reason for this meeting is to discuss the contents of a trunk that Sadie put up for auction. The trunk had contents that upon investigation have been shown to have value. Mr. Webb has provided me with a complete list of the contents of the trunk, which includes items and papers that have been unmistakably linked to the American Revolution."

Earle cut in, "We just want to know how much it is all worth." Sadie gave him a stare that could have melted stone and he said no more.

Lawyer Larsen continued. "Mr. Webb has generously said he wants to give all the contents back to Mrs. Woodruff. Greta has said she would like to keep the trunk itself."

John Henry now grunted to show his disapproval and received his own stare from Sadie.

"As I was saying," said Larsen, "Greta volunteered to pay what the true value of the trunk might be. Sadie has said she does not want any additional funds for the trunk." Both Earle and John Henry looked wide-eyed at this, but they held their peace.

"There was some men's clothing that has been identified to be from the eighteenth century. There were some letters and newspaper clippings and some books that I believe are of interest here. There were also some documents that we will discuss when my agent arrives. Perhaps the most valuable object found in the trunk is a Bible." Sadie now smiled at this information. The nephews looked at Lawyer Larsen in disbelief.

Gramps said, "That Bible was printed by Robert Aitken in 1782. We were extremely pleased when we found it in the trunk."

"Yes, as it turns out, Mr. Webb, it is one of the rarest of books. Only about forty copies are known today. Sadie has decided to donate the Bible to the Museum of the Bible in Washington, D.C." Both nephews jumped from their seats.

Earle almost shouted. "What? You can't do that! A book that rare must be worth thousands. We could put it up for bid and make a mint." Sadie only smiled as if she expected this reaction from her nearest relatives.

"Please sit down, Mr. Brubaker. Your aunt has every right to donate the Bible to the museum. It is a valuable item but also has significance and meaning to many people. The public will benefit from the donation."

At that moment Marguerite returned with a tray of teacups and began to offer them to everyone. I picked up my plate of cookies and began to pass it around. Earle declined a cookie. John Henry took two and everyone else took one. Soon everyone but Earle was sipping tea and munching on a cookie. Earle sat with his arms folded across his chest and very much resembled a little boy who was pouting because he was being punished.

The doorbell rang and Marguerite went to let Detective Donny Dolittle in. Earle and John Henry gasped at his appearance.

"What are you doing here, Dolittle?" Earle asked in a voice the neighbors could hear.

"I just came to make my report," the detective calmly replied.

Earle angrily said, "When I want your report, you will come to me privately."

"I don't work for you anymore, Mr. Brubaker. I work for Mr. Larsen and will make my report to the group as he has requested."

"You can't do that. We have a contract," Earle shouted while John Henry reached for a third cookie.

"Our contract ended when your check bounced. Mr. Larsen has asked me to do some research for him and I am now prepared to make my report."

The lawyer now stepped in, "Mr. Brubaker, let's allow Mr. Dolittle to make his report. I believe he has some facts that we will all benefit from hearing. Go ahead, Mr. Dolittle."

The lawyer walked back to his chair and the detective was now standing in the center of the room with some papers in his hand. He had the attention of everyone in the room except John Henry, who was motioning for Marguerite to fill his teacup again while he ate his fourth cookie.

"Let me start by saying that you were right in your suspicions that there was something of value in the trunk, Mr. Brubaker." Earle seemed pleased with this admission. "The trunk belonged to Robert Townsend, who lived on Long Island. Townsend was a Quaker who lived during the traumatic times of the Revolution. He was a businessman who worked in New York City, which was occupied for most of the war by the British. It wasn't discovered until 1930 that Townsend was a spy for General Washington. Apparently, his handwriting matched that of the spy known as Culper junior. After the war, Townsend seemed to withdraw from life. There was speculation that he had a love affair that ended and left him in despair. The housekeeper had a child who was named Robert Townsend Jr. There is a lot of uncertainty about this child. He may have belonged to Robert, but years later Solomon Townsend said the boy was actually the offspring of another brother named William. Much of this is conjecture, but the housekeeper's son does not appear to have been sired by Robert. We will probably never know the cause of Mr. Townsend's despair."

Earle couldn't hold back any longer. "Come on, Dolittle. I am not interested in the romances of someone two hundred years ago. What does all this have to do with the trunk?" At the same time John Henry gazed longingly at the now empty cookie plate. Only two ant-sized crumbs remained.

"We are coming to that, Mr. Brubaker. If you will just bear with me a little longer, I think it will all make sense." The detective looked at Sadie, who nodded for him to continue. "After the war, Townsend never claimed any reward." Both Earle and John Henry's eyes seemed to light up at the word 'reward.'

"He just settled into his family home in Oyster Bay with his sister Sally. Like I said, no one knew that Townsend had actually helped Washington by his espionage activities. No one knew except perhaps Washington and his spy chief, Benjamin Tallmadge."

The detective paused here as if to make sure the group was adequately prepared for what he would say next.

Aunt Sadie chimed in, "Now don't stop there, Dick Tracy. Fill us in before the next presidential election. What did Washington do?"

"Actually, Mrs. Woodruff, Washington never rewarded Townsend. It was probably because he never met him personally. Townsend never sought him out either. He never even applied for a pension while many others did. It was for that reason that Townsend was more or less forgotten until 1817. Washington himself had passed away in 1799, but his spy chief was still around. Benjamin Tallmadge was still serving in Congress in 1817, and that's when it happened." Once again he paused.

Once again Earle's patience ran out. "Blast it, Dolittle! Tell us what happened!"

"After the war, pensions were given to soldiers who served in the Continental Army. Land grants were also given as a reward to those who served. Tallmadge was a member of Congress when the three men who had caught the British spy chief John Andre and exposed Benedict Arnold applied for an expansion to their pension. It appears that Tallmadge was against the pension expansion but remembered that Townsend had never gotten anything."

It was Gramps's turn to interrupt. "So that letter we found was from Tallmadge to Townsend thanking him for his service? What about the document? Is it really genuine? Is it really worth something after all these years?"

"I was coming to that, Mr. Webb. The document, like everything else in the trunk, appears to be genuine. I think we will have to have it examined by other experts, but as of now we have no reason to doubt its validity."

I could almost bust now and spoke up, "That document looked like a land grant. I think it designated 500 acres to Mr. Townsend."

Now both Earle and John Henry's jaws seemed to drop, and everyone said at once, "500 acres of land!"

Lawyer Larsen joined in again. He held up the document for all to see. "Yes, this document is the real deal. It looks like a land grant for 500 acres with coordinates on Long Island, New York."

Earle jumped out of his seat again and shouted, "Eureka and hot tamales! We did it! Five hundred acres on Long Island! Do you know how much that is worth? Millions! It's worth millions! Dolittle and Larsen, I could kiss you both, but I won't."

Once again Larsen tried to restore order. "Gentlemen, it may not be that easy. We have been doing some checking on the coordinates of the 500 acres. Back in 1817 it was farmland but not any more. It's a housing development for the most part. It's all developed property. People are living there. A hundred acres of it is part of a city park."

I now asked what I thought was the obvious key question. "How does that land grant pass from Robert Townsend to Aunt Sadie?"

"Ah yes, my dear. You have asked the question that everyone living on that property today and all their lawyers will be asking. It's probably the most important question of the day. You remember that Robert Townsend was a bachelor? If those 500 acres belonged to him, how does he pass it on? Specifically, how does it go to Mrs. Woodruff?"

Earle added, "And to her relatives."

Detective Donny Dolittle cleared his throat at this point. "Once again," he said, "I have the answer. Mr. Webb, you will recall there were three papers in the small box you found. One was a blank page."

"Yes, it seemed odd that a blank page would be kept along with an important document and a letter," said Gramps.

"I have been working on that blank page," said the detective. "The historical record tells us that Washington's spy ring had to use invisible ink." The whole group that was gathered seemed to sense where the detective was going with this. "I applied a reagent to the blank page and sure enough, there was writing on it."

"Out with it man! What did you find?" Earle shouted.

"It was a last will and testament written by Robert Townsend. He gave all of his property to his housekeeper, Mary Banvard. I have been working on the housekeeper angle for some time now. In all probability, she was the mother of the child who was named Robert Townsend after our spy Robert Townsend. She eventually left the Townsend home, which was called Raynham Hall, and married a man named Josiah Woodruff."

Aunt Sadie suddenly gasped. "Josiah Woodruff was Uncle Eb's ancestor, I believe. I heard Uncle Eb talk about him on more than one occasion. Well, I'll be switched."

"So you see, ladies and gentlemen, Mrs. Woodruff is indeed the heir to Robert Townsend of Raynham Hall in Oyster Bay. I must caution everyone, though, that a will and land grant like this won't be easy to process and lay claim to what appears to be rightfully Aunt Sadie's. It could wind up in court battles for years."

Earle once again felt like he was in the driver's seat. "It won't be that difficult, Larsen. The way I figure it 500 acres of land on Long Island must be worth at least a million dollars an acre. That means 500 million dollars. We will have to cut some deals with some folks and then hire some sharp lawyers to sue the rest. Even with the exorbitant legal fees, we should be able to clear 250 million dollars by the time we are through."

"Hold on now, Earle Brubaker. You are forgetting one small little detail."

"What's that, Aunt Sadie?"

"None of this belongs to you. It all belongs to me."

There was a ten-second pause while Earle shifted gears. "Now Aunt Sadie, you know we would be the best ones to handle your affairs. We only have your interests at heart, and we are your nearest relatives, after all."

"My interests, my foot! You boys ignored me for years until you started to think dollar signs and figured you should come running over."

"That's not true, Sadie. You just never seemed to be hospitable to us. You kept to yourself and wouldn't return my phone calls."

"You didn't call me for about ten years and then all of a sudden you thought I was ready to die so you started calling."

"Aunt Sadie, I am hurt by what you just said."

"Let me ask you this, Earle Brubaker, if I didn't have any money besides what it takes to bury me, would you take me into your house to live and care for me until I died?

"We certainly would, Aunt Sadie. You know we would." Earle put on his most sincere face and motioned to John Henry who nodded his agreement.

Sadie pushed the lever on the wheelchair and moved forward to where Lawyer Larsen was sitting. "May I see that document, Milton?"

"Of course you may, Sadie. The land is yours and the document is yours." He handed her the document, and she moved the lever on the wheelchair to return to her position under the light beside the fire. She held the document in her hands for a long time. The room was silent as Sadie studied the document and mulled over what she should do. After a few moments she raised her eyes and looked about the room.

"Okay, I believe I know what I should do in this situation." All eyes were on Aunt Sadie. "First of all, I am giving the fifty dollars back to Mr. Webb and Greta. She can keep the trunk. I haven't had this much excitement in years, and I am thankful to them. I only hope you two can bring me some cookies once in a while." Gramps and I both smiled and nodded our agreement.

"Second, I really do want to have a better relationship with you two Brubaker boys. I am going to give you the copy of *Common Sense* by Thomas Paine found in the box. It is not as valuable as the Bible was, and I know it is really a political treatise. Nevertheless, I am thinking of it as an object lesson. You boys need some common sense in how to treat people without expecting to profit by it financially.

"But, Aunt Sadie," the brothers started to protest. She held up a hand to stop them.

"You say it's not my money you are interested in. You say you would take care of me whether I had money or not."

"We sure would, Aunt Sadie." The nephews nodded to one another and back to Aunt Sadie.

She held up the document. "This piece of paper says I am entitled to 500 acres of land worth millions of dollars." The nephews continued to nod. "This paper means that I could move people out of their homes and take ownership of a public park where children play today. You boys say you will take care of me whether I have money or not." The nephews once again nodded.

Everyone was quiet now. We were all staring at Aunt Sadie. She was staring at the document and then looked over her glasses right at me. "What do you think, dearie? What should I do?" I was dumbfounded. My parents and Gramps and Gram would often ask my opinion, but this was different. I swallowed hard and wanted to think of something amazing to say. What words of wisdom could I offer? I then realized it was obvious. I cleared my throat and said, "Aunt Sadie, whatever you decide, I think you're tops."

Her eyes were shining now and a big grin covered her face. "That's all I wanted to hear, dearie."

Sadie took a long moment to look around the room. "All I can say is we shall see." Every eye grew wide as Sadie turned toward the fireplace. "Yes, we shall see." Her hand fed the yellowed document into the colorful flame.

Afterword

The American Revolution opened with hostility in New England at the Battles of Lexington and Concord on April 19, 1775. The colonists went on to push the British out of Boston, and George Washington was selected as commander of the colonial armies. He rightly judged that the British would soon go to New York to set up operations for war. He moved his army there in preparation.

The seeds of the American Revolution had been planted more than a decade earlier during the French and Indian War, which ended in 1763. That war was called the Seven Years War back in Europe, but it was primarily fought in the colonial territories over conflicting claims by France and England. Colonists fought alongside British regulars against the French. George Washington participated as a young man of twenty-one. The French were building forts on territory the Virginia colony claimed. Washington carried a message from Virginia Governor Dinwiddie to the French commandant for him to cease and withdraw. On that mission Washington walked about and made notes of the French fort's position and strength. Washington reported his findings back to Governor Dinwiddie and learned firsthand the value of information gained. He would not forget that lesson.

Britain successfully defended its territorial claims and a treaty was signed in Paris that ended the French and Indian War. The hostilities were ended, but it did not end the animosity between the two superpowers. The war also left a financial burden, and Britain had a plan to relieve that burden. The war had been over the colonies, and now the colonies should pay for it. Britain began to levy a series of taxes on the colonies that they in turn bitterly resented. The colonies had no representation in Parliament and no avenue to express their grievances. The phrase "no taxation without representation" was coined. Americans began to boycott British goods and smuggle other goods into the colonies to avoid paying the disputed taxes.

The ill will between the colonies and the Crown now began to boil over into outright hostility. This led to the Boston Tea Party and the Battles of Lexington and Concord. The smell of gunpowder was now in the air and there was no turning back. The British Redcoats were forced out of Boston, and Washington was made commander of the army. He traveled to New York suspecting it to be the most likely target for the British to invade. He was right, but they soon forced his evacuation. He left with the determination that in order to return he would need to be updated with information on his enemy's strength and position. He wanted to send a spy into New York. Thus was the ill-fated mission of Nathan Hale born.

The historical portion of this novel has revolved around a spy ring that Washington used to gather information in New York preparing to reclaim that territory. Washington formed the Culper spy ring and often supported it with his own personal finances. The Patriot spies risked their lives for very little monetary gain. This was contrasted with those who performed espionage for the Crown. British spies would dig deeply into the pockets of the Crown and performed little service in return.

This novel has been an attempt to blend history with mystery. In the belief that history is stranger than fiction, the historical characters and events have been portrayed as accurately as feasible. The conversations between characters are a product of imagination but represent the events which did take place.

For example Tallmadge was the last of the war veterans who did serve in Congress. The three highwaymen did petition Congress for an expansion of their pension and Tallmadge spoke against granting it to them. Robert Townsend was Culper junior but that was not discovered until the twentieth century. He and Woodhull and others did not receive a pension. They had faced the gravest of dangers for a period of time and would have been rewarded as Nathan Hale was by the British if caught.

It should also be noted that some historical characters and situations are somewhat clouded. We have portrayed Robert Townsend as being a Quaker, but this may not be the case. His mother was not and his father was at best a liberal Quaker. He was certainly influenced by the book *Common Sense* and his background was tied to the Quaker beliefs.

The identity of Agent 355 is a mystery that may never be solved. Brian Kilmeade's paperback edition of *George Washington's Secret Six* goes into a discussion of possible ladies, but also shows why they may not be the agent. In this account, we simply portray her as a Patriot from a Loyalist family. She had connections with British officers and citizens of New York and could gather information. The romantic connection between Townsend and Agent 355 has been suggested before and may have been the case.

Although Aunt Sadie is fictional as well as Greta and Gramps, we can imagine events after the final parlor scene. Her nephews were more than a little upset with her but things began to change. There was no longer the promise of 250 million dollars coupled with the headaches of lawsuits. She promised them half of her existing assets on the condition that they each find a job and begin to handle their finances in a responsible way.

Gramps helped John Henry to find a job in a bakery for which he was very grateful. He also gained about twenty pounds in six months. Gramps helped Earle find a job in an antique store where he was constantly on the lookout for items of hidden value. They began to visit Sadie on a regular basis and even started mowing her lawn. Lawyer Larsen was tasked with checking on their financial status to make sure they were paying their bills.

Greta and Gramps went to visit Sadie on numerous occasions. She became an unofficial part of the Webb family.

*　　　*　　　*

Further reading on the history of the Culper spy ring could include,

George Washington's Secret Six: The Spy Ring that Saved the American Revolution by Brian Kilmeade and Don Yaeger (New York: Sentinel, 2016)

Washington's Spies: The Story of America's First Spy Ring by Alexander Rose (New York: Bantam DELL,2006)

Nathan Hale:The Life and Death of America's First Spy by M. William Phelps (Lebanon, NH, ForeEdge, 2008)

Lafayette: Hero of Two Worlds by Olivier Bernier (New York: Dutton, 1983, Kindle edition, New Word City, 2017)

The Notorious Benedict Arnold: A True Story of Adventure, Heroism, and Treachery by Steve Sheinkin (New York: Flash Point, 2010)

Many thanks are due to the team of people who helped produce this book. I, alone, am responsible for errors that may be displayed in the work. Kathy Deselle spent hours trying to correct my mistakes. Allyson Wilkins did the drawings which are found within. Charity Parker did the cover and formatting. Reads and critiques were done by Erin DeMelo, Arlene Pastore, and my grandkids Violet Wilkins, Caleb Wilkins, Abby and Sophie DeMelo.

Made in the USA
Middletown, DE
29 May 2019